AG

Dane Curtis had always been like a brother to Helen. But now that she was living with him she found that her feelings towards him were hardly that of a sister. Especially when the beautiful Marina Cole was around!

AGE OF CONSENT

BY
VICTORIA GORDON

MILLS & BOON LIMITED
15–16 BROOK'S MEWS
LONDON W1A 1DR

*First published in Great Britain 1985
by Mills & Boon Limited*

© Victoria Gordon 1985

*Australian copyright 1985
Philippine copyright 1985
This edition 1985*

ISBN 0 263 75062 0

*Set in Monophoto Times 10 on 11 pt.
01–0685 – 57940*

*Made and printed in Great Britain by
Richard Clay (The Chaucer Press) Ltd,
Bungay, Suffolk*

For Helen-Fred, it must be.

CHAPTER ONE

THE voice on the telephone was as welcome as it was unexpected, rumbling like distant, wind-driven surf and assaulting her ear with neither greeting nor salutation to soften the assault.

Welcome? Yes, oh yes! But so totally unexpected and so direct in its inquisition that Helen couldn't have a hope of dissembling, didn't have any chance at all to cover up.

'Well?'

That was his second remark; the first had been a brusque, 'What the hell's going on up there? And don't bother trying to think up some piddly little lie; you can't even lie effectively by letter, much less over the 'phone.'

'Oh, Dane.' It was all she could push past the lump of raw emotion that threatened to choke her, but it was enough to prime the well-spring of tears that flooded from eyes like soft grey velvet.

'If I had my way, I'd have paddled some sense into you years ago,' was the harsh reply, but Helen knew the harshness was only a vocal disguise for his own emotions, a tool deliberately used to ferret out the blunt, direct answers he needed.

Normally she'd have traded him flippant reply for brutally direct question, both of them taking pleasure from the exchange, but now ... now she was too close to the end of her rope for any such show of false courage. Blinking back her tears, she tried to choose the words, knowing even as she did so that it was a waste of time. She couldn't fool Dane Curtis, not even over the 'phone.

Couldn't ... and wasn't. She could tell that much by

the softening of his voice as he spoke again, not bothering to await her reply to his last barrage.

'Come on . . . out with it. I already know you've been retrenched, but we've both been there before without all this trauma. So what else? Pregnant? Jilted? All hung up over some bloke with a wife and six kids at home? Or something really serious?'

It was so typical of him that she had to laugh past her tears. Nobody but Dane would . . . could . . . be so honestly caring and yet so easily able to dismiss the seriousness of issues most young women would consider very serious indeed.

'What if I said all three . . . and more?' she countered bravely, knowing the answer before hearing it from a voice she'd not heard in more than two long years.

'There isn't much left except being broke and knowing it'll be twins or triplets,' he replied with a quiet chuckle. 'And even then I'm sure we could find some solution. If that was the problem, which it isn't . . . at least not totally. So what is it, love?'

And now that voice was muted, softened by a love she'd never questioned, never doubted in all the six years she'd known him.

'Well I'm not pregnant, he isn't married, and thinking back on it, even the jilting part doesn't really surprise me,' she said, playing for time to extract the exact words, the right words to try and explain. As if it were really necessary.

'So you're broke and out of a job . . . again. And too stubborn and independent to ask for help, as usual,' he said. 'Sometimes I wonder about you, child. And I suppose you're up to your ears in debt, too, or is that next week?'

'Probably,' Helen replied, then went on to explain at some length exactly what the trouble was. It wasn't easy, and indeed she couldn't have explained it to anyone but Dane, not even to her mother. Least of all to her mother, who would only see it as yet another lever in her incessant campaign to draw Helen back to the destructive, emotion-baited trap of the family home.

No, she could never explain to her mother the soul-destroying trauma of being retrenched—never fired!—from four different jobs in less than two years. Always, or so she'd thought at first, because of the traditional last on-first off policies common to the journalistic media throughout Australia.

At first she'd accepted the situation far better than the first time she'd been retrenched, five-and-a-half years before when some distant management decision had chopped down the weekly suburban paper on which both she and Dane had been employed.

That very first time she'd been stunned for days, simply unable to accept the situation, and then unable not to feel that in some way she, personally, was to blame.

It had been Dane and his wife Vivian who'd pulled her through that catastrophe, first with gentle kindness and finally with brutal directness, but always with a genuine liking, loving, sincerity.

Dane, then in his early thirties and with one foot perched precariously on the tight-rope leading to his present career as a successful novelist, had accepted the verdict philosophically, fought to find Helen a place elsewhere in the organisation and then haughtily refused one for himself, choosing instead to go back free-lancing so he'd have time to work on his novels.

'I can afford to play that kind of game; you can't,' he'd told her, insisting she take the alternative job at least until something came along that she liked better.

She'd done so, still dazed by the suddenness of it all, still reeling with the shock and the horrible, empty feeling of being useless, inadequate. Being retrenched, at nineteen, from the second job she'd ever held in her life was, she'd thought at the time, absolutely the worst of catastrophes. Now she was twenty-five, and, it seemed, no less vulnerable than before.

It was that vulnerability, that yawning, empty feeling of uselessness that threatened her now, and she poured out her feelings into the receptive ear that was so many years, so many miles away now, and yet so comfortingly close.

Four jobs gone in two years. She'd been unable to attend Vivian's funeral the year before because she'd been out of work and broke and on the move. Dane, not having heard from her in months, was simply unable to contact her until the next time she wrote.

Once, she'd gone home, seeing in her mother's pleas for help some logic to returning to the country town where she'd grown up. But the pleas hadn't been real, or at least not real in the sense of having any validity. They'd been only her mother trying a new tack in her life-long bid to control Helen's life, to hold her at the controllable, pliable age of sixteen. She'd left again after a fortnight, feeling a frighteningly disturbing combination of hatred and love and pity for the woman who'd borne her and whom, she knew, loved her despite being unable to show it in any fashion Helen could accept.

But this last retrenchment, especially combined with the immediate lack of interest on the part of a man she thought she loved, had proved to be very nearly the final straw.

Which was why she hadn't mentioned either in her letter to Dane a few days earlier. Instead, she'd written her usual quarterly letter, filled with trivia and cunningly worded to disguise the fears. So cunningly worded, obviously, that he'd simply ignored it, choosing instead to read between the lines and begin his own investigation. It would, she realised, have been done very discreetly, very subtly, through tenuous links between contacts she probably didn't even know he had.

And very swiftly, considering he'd picked up the essence within days, with her in Brisbane and him, she presumed, on his farm in Tasmania.

Did he know, as well, that she'd be without a place to live by next week when the owner of the flat she was keeping returned from six months overseas? He hadn't, but seemed hardly surprised.

'Nothing that happens to you surprises me,' he replied. 'I knew from the very beginning that you were a walking disaster area; what I didn't expect was that you'd never grow out of it.'

Helen's reply was a mixture of laughter and tears. She, too, remembered that beginning, the day she'd walked in, green as grass, to start her first day's work on the short-lived suburban weekly. She'd been young, innocent, awash with the incredible naïvety which only a convent or a small Australian country town can produce, and broke. Anxious to be accepted, she'd joined the rest of the staff for beer and sandwiches at noon, worked right through until the banks had all closed, and found herself sheepishly admitting at closing time that she had two dollars to her name and hadn't got round to finding a flat.

The remark, so ludicrously innocent in retrospect, had drawn expressions of sympathy from everyone but Dane, who had merely stared at her for an eternity through cynical, ice-blue eyes. Eyes that seemed to have seen everything, their ice-blue colour shot with flashes of amber but none, it seemed, of sympathy.

And yet it had been he who'd muttered softly, 'Not to worry. I suppose we can manage one more at table tonight and find you a bed until you're settled.'

Then, taking her silence for acceptance, he'd phoned Vivian at her office and warned of the impending invasion. That was the first Helen had even known of his marital status. Since that night the Curtises had practically adopted her.

Dane and Vivian had seen her through tragic love affairs, traffic accidents, traumas with her own family and a seemingly never-ending chain of job changes as she transferred for more money, a different challenge, a different boss.

Their discipline of her life-style had been low-key to the point of being non-existent, except professionally. There, both of them journalists of long-standing, they had insisted on a true professional attitude. Advice of any sort was freely given but without any strings attached. If she ignored the advice, as she often did, there were no hassles, no complaints, and no 'I told you so' when she was proved wrong in her decisions.

After that first year, their paths had crossed less and less frequently, what with moves to various different cities on both parts. But Helen and Dane had kept in touch by letter, with him letting her set the pace of the interchange, writing as regularly as she chose to do.

And during the past three years, at least, she'd chosen to write less and less often. At first it was because she knew that it was imperative she become her own person, develop her own individuality, solve her own problems. But latterly, especially since Vivian's untimely death in a traffic accident, it was because Helen could all too easily wish for herself a closer role in his life, and that wouldn't work at all.

'Well it doesn't sound any worse than usual to me,' he was saying now. 'Although I suppose you're wallowing in self-pity and totally convinced that it's the end of the world.'

'I am not!' she denied stoutly, lying through her teeth and knowing they both realised that.

'You couldn't lie straight in bed,' he growled. 'What happened to that job you mentioned a few months ago? Somebody leading you down the garden path again, as usual?'

Helen winced at the accusation. Much as she fancied herself the hardened, cynical, world-wise journalist that Dane, himself, was, she had to admit that in many ways she seemed doomed to face life with her naïvety as a fragile, intimidating shield.

'No, I think it was the economy that did that one in,' she finally replied. And felt the tears spring up again.

'It's always the economy; you ought to know that, living where you are. Or has Tasmania finally got away from being the worst state in Australia for unemployment?'

'There's more good jobs than good journalists,' he replied, ignoring her question as she'd expected. And then, unexpectedly, 'Which always makes me wonder why there are so many lousy ones hanging on to them.'

Helen was honestly astonished at that. It was so totally at odds with the convictions he'd expressed in years past, usually in the process of convincing her not to worry because of having been retrenched or because her current job wasn't going as she'd hoped.

But he was continuing before she could reply. 'Anyway, it doesn't much matter at this point. So what about the man in it all? Or were you just throwing him in as a red herring?'

Again, Helen winced, knowing even as she began to explain about Bryce what the reaction would be. Even just hearing Dane's no-nonsense voice, she realised herself that she'd been a victim of her own naïvety once again. Bryce, as second in charge of a public relations firm, had blatantly used his extensive charm to sway Helen, although—and here she was firm in her assertions—it had been only in a personal sense that she'd been swayed. Her journalistic scruples had been too firmly moulded to be at risk.

Dane's reply was scathingly acidic. 'Oh, of course. And I suppose he was also a paid-in-full AJA member, so he could claim to be a fellow journalist as well.'

Helen didn't get a chance to reply. Nor did she need to really listen to know what was coming next; she knew only too well his opinion of public relations people being allowed as members of the Australian Journalists' Association.

'. . . total contradiction in terms,' he was saying. 'Like hookers in a convent. And besides, even if he was a proper journalist—haven't I always told you to stay away from other journalists? No sane woman would get involved with one; they're all bastards.'

Helen sighed. Damn him! He knew as well as she did that for a working journalist, especially a female one, about the only men available were other journalists. Nobody else could abide the ridiculous working hours, much less the dedicated work habits that were required for success. Or, she mused idly, the lack of it, especially in her own case.

'Did you 'phone all the way up here just to harangue about that?' she finally demanded. 'Because if you did . . .'

'It's my 'phone bill and I'll harangue about anything I please,' he interjected. 'But no, that's not what I 'phoned for, so stop trying to change the subject. What I want to know is what you're going to do now.'

'I . . . I don't honestly know,' she admitted, realising even as she spoke that she was making the admission to herself as well, and not pleased with that final acceptance.

'That'd be right,' was the dry rejoinder. 'I knew I should have sold you into white slavery while you were young enough to be worth something.' And then, as if he realised that comment had come a shade too close to the bone, 'You been doing any riding lately, or have you given up horses in favour of jumped-up advertising types?'

'I haven't been on a horse in about a year,' she replied wistfully, and realised even as she said it that her entire journalistic career had been at the expense of dealing with horses.

Helen's childhood had been spent on a property in central New South Wales, and even after the family's move to town after her father's death, she'd continued to maintain an interest in riding. But she'd sold her horses, finally, to pay off some debt or another, and the business of her profession had since then contrived to keep her from having the time for horses ever since.

'Why did you ask that?' she queried, suddenly suspicious. Dane seldom asked questions without some motive, especially innocuous questions like that one.

But her own question was now ignored. 'Not much going for jobs in Brisbane, I gather,' he was saying. 'And from what I hear it's no better down south, unless you fancy shifting to one of the country papers.'

'I'd rather starve,' Helen scoffed, exaggerating somewhat, but no less emphatic for all that. She'd started her career in a country paper, and to go back to one now, unless in some executive position, would be only a step backward in her own eyes.

'How's your car going?' Again, a seemingly innocuous question, but she knew, this time, what he was getting at.

'I sold it last week, and I suspect you knew that,' she replied calmly. 'Which is why . . . for the moment . . . I haven't any debts, thank you.'

'Well, that's a change,' he chuckled. 'No job, no money, no place to live, but at least no debts. You're improving, love. Usually you've got all four problems at once.'

Dane's refusal to take the matter seriously was now beginning to annoy Helen, especially as his call had been sufficient already to make her take stock of her problems with considerably more seriousness than he was exhibiting.

'Did you 'phone up just to rub my nose in it?' she demanded angrily. 'Because if you did . . .'

'I 'phoned to see if I could be of help, you silly little twit,' was the abrasive reply. 'And just as well, from the sound of things.'

'I didn't,' she interrupted with unnecessary vigour, 'ask for any help, did I?'

'Not in so many words, perhaps,' he replied with infuriating calm. 'Although from the amount of tripe you stuck into your last letter, it wouldn't take more than an idiot to guess . . .'

'Will you stop it!' she cried. Angry now. Genuinely angry despite knowing full well he was deliberately goading her, forcing her up from the pit of her own self-pity by methods he knew would work, however temporarily.

'If you insist,' he replied blandly. 'But not before I get to the point of this call, which is costing me heaps of money, in case you're interested.'

'Well then get to the point,' she snapped. 'For somebody who's supposed to be a professional communicator, you beat around the bush worse than anybody I've ever known.'

'There, see how much better you feel,' he laughed. 'It's always much easier when you've got somebody you can shout at, isn't it?'

'Just be glad that's all I can do to you,' she muttered, anger only partially mollified. 'If you were here, I'd . . .'

It was his turn to interrupt. 'Got it backwards as usual,' he jeered. 'How about if *you* were *here*?'

'I'd give you a knuckle sandwich, for starters,' she cried, only half understanding and too angry still to think straight. It was only when he didn't immediately reply that the implication of his question began to sink in. And with the implication . . . caution!

'What are you getting at?' she hissed, suspicious, now. 'Did your housekeeper up and quit you or something?'

He merely chuckled, the sound a friendly, somehow-secure rumbling over the 'phone. 'I'd hardly be calling you if that was the case,' he said softly. 'The only thing worse than your housekeeping is your cooking.'

Helen tried to ignore the truth of the sarcasm. 'Well what, then? Surely you're not looking for a secretary.'

The chuckle became a laugh. 'I lied,' he said. 'Your typing is worse than your cooking, even, presuming, of course, that anybody would dignify it by actually calling it *typing*.' And he laughed again at the gasp that statement provoked.

Then there was silence, a silence which Helen attempted to use wisely, shifting her mind back through their conversation for a hint.

'Chauffeur?'

'The way you drive? Not on your life. I value my tired old bones too much for that, thanks.'

'You're not being very helpful.'

'I'm not trying to be.'

'Well then you'll have to change, because I honestly can't guess. Especially after you've rejected almost every potential virtue I have remaining.'

He sighed, then spoke in a deliberately soft, enticing voice. 'Maybe I just want you for my mistress. You're still not bad looking.'

Helen giggled. It was an old line, used even when Vivian was alive, and her response was always the same.

'You're too old and not rich enough, and besides . . .' she halted there with a gasp, realising how hurtful it would be to continue, how hurtful it must be anyway. *Vivian wouldn't approve.* That was the clincher in the reply, and she'd said it without speaking the words, without thinking.

'Oh Dane, I'm so sorry,' Helen cried. 'I just didn't think.'

'Forget it. Besides, *now* she might very well approve, although the rest still holds good. You're too young and I'm not rich enough,' he responded, no hint of pain in his voice. But it was there, Helen knew. Despite his hazing, he'd loved his wife beyond all imagining, and probably, almost certainly, loved her memory equally.

'All right,' she said, 'but I do wish you'd be serious for a change. This call must be costing you a fortune and I . . . I still don't know why you called.'

'Because I worry about you. You know that,' he replied. 'And because you're such a bad liar, I now know what I called to find out. Things are getting close to rock bottom, eh?'

'I'll survive,' she replied quickly, hoping the words would cover the instinctive catch in her throat at his accuracy.

'Be easier down here. Why not fly down for a holiday and take some time to straighten yourself out?'

He'd said it so casually that anyone else might have been fooled, but Helen knew Dane Curtis better than that. Still, she paused to think before replying.

'I thought we agreed a long time ago that I should learn to fly on my own?' she replied cautiously, half expecting a sarcastic reply concerning how poorly she'd managed.

'What does that have to do with the price of beer?' he replied. Casual ... gentle ... too casual.

'Enough that you should know I couldn't possibly come down there to sponge off you,' she replied. 'Not even if I wanted to.'

'If you wanted to, I damned well wouldn't let you,' he growled. 'And if you were that desperate, I wouldn't have 'phoned; I'd have come up to collect you personally.'

Which, Helen realised only too well, he very well would have. Only then it wouldn't have been a case of sponging, but one of being whipped back into shape the hard way. Dane was a firm believer in the theory that friends didn't have to be polite, and indeed often shouldn't be. He'd levelled some harsh truisms at her in the past, and wouldn't hesitate to do so again.

'Well I'm not that desperate, although I have to admit I'm getting close,' she responded, already easing back from the brink through the simple knowledge that somebody out there really cared. Somebody special, important, and secure enough in their relationship to be totally straight with her.

'So why not come? Sure as hell there's nothing there to hold you, or is there?' And now there was that probing stiletto in his voice, undisguised and irrefutable.

'And do what?' she replied, half angry again. 'There hasn't been a journo's job advertised from Tasmania in nearly a year, you don't want me to cook, or clean, or type, or . . . well, you know, Some of which, by the way, is really very unfair, because since you last remember I've learned to cook quite well and my housekeeping is at least as good as yours.'

'But your typing's still no good; I've got the proof of that,' he said, tactfully ignoring the final possibility, to Helen's great relief. 'Besides, I'm offering you a rest, not a new career. But, if you insist on something useful to do, there's plenty of work here. Provided you haven't forgotten how.'

'Forgotten how? What on earth are you talking about?' she demanded, curious now, but angry because she knew only too well she was curious only because he was arranging things that way.

'Work, my child. Good, honest, out-of-doors stuff, like feeding the chooks and the ducks and the geese, and slopping the hogs, and herding the goats.'

He paused momentarily at her honest gasp of amazement, then continued with a hint of chuckle still burbling in his voice. 'Of course I wouldn't dare let you loose with a chain saw, but maybe I can get one of the neighbour's little kids to teach you to drive the tractor. And you ought to know all about lambing and such, having been raised with it . . .'

Helen's laugh, almost hysterical with relief, cut him off there. 'You want me to be a farm-hand!' she cried, not sure whether to laugh or cry.

Dane's voice, when she'd sobered sufficiently to allow him a reply, was totally nonplussed. 'I believe,' he said pompously—deliberately so—'the proper term is *jillaroo*.'

She laughed again, finding the whole idea so absurd, so ludicrous, so . . . tempting, despite her certainty that Dane was joking.

'Jillaroos get horses to ride,' she said then. 'Do I get a horse?'

'Well . . . sort of,' and for the first time she realised there was a tentative note in that familiar voice. And a hint that he just might be serious, too.

'What does that mean?' she demanded. 'You do know what a horse is? Four legs? A thing you put a saddle on? For riding?'

'Don't be cheeky.' But there was that faint note of hesitation. Only Helen was now caught up in the game, and although she felt it, should have been warned, she couldn't resist a snappy reply.

'Not cheeky, just checking the facts—like you taught me,' she replied. She still wasn't sure if he was being serious, and really thought it quite unlikely, but still . . . 'And that's the facts; I want something to ride. Doesn't have to be a flash Arabian or anything, but something at least fit to throw a saddle on. That, or no deal!'

'Done!' And it was so quick, so definite, that she found herself holding her breath, waiting for the trap to spring. But all he said next was, 'I'll pick you up at the airport.'

And he hung up.

Helen sat for a moment, holding the humming receiver in her suddenly-nerveless fingers and wondering if that insane conversation had really occurred. And if it had, was there anything to it? Or was he just playing silly games?

No, she decided, putting down the receiver in the same instant. Dane wouldn't play games like that. Never would he involve himself in anything hurtful. And yet . . . what?

Rising, she strode into the bathroom and stood staring idly into the mirror, her imagination toying at the transformation which would be required to return her to a simple country-girl image. It was difficult, after nearly six years in the cities.

Facing her was a tastefully, if not expensively dressed

figure, not a bad figure by most tastes, either. She wasn't what anyone would call really slim, but the youthful pudginess had given way to a reasonable shapeliness. Good legs, anyway. Her hair was her real nemesis. Medium-length, the colour of good bush honey, it looked really nice only when she could spend the time to keep it so, but the once she'd cut it short, the result had been disastrous with her features.

Wide-set grey eyes above a nose that carried a narrow, high bridge—the result of falling off a horse when she was younger—dark, reasonably shaped eyebrows, slightly pudgy cheeks and the wide, even-toothed smile that she knew was her main saving grace. When she smiled, her entire face lit up, according to Dane and one or two others favoured with that smile.

Small-breasted, but not unreasonably so, and with a tidy, narrow waist. And below that, the one aspect of her figure she'd give almost anything to change and probably never could.

Dane had once called it her 'horsewoman's rump' and had laughingly chided her for being born a hundred years too late. 'In the last century, love, you'd have been the envy of all the high-class ladies, with a built-in bustle like that,' he'd said, and taken the sting out of the remark by adding, 'and damned few women today could match the way you look in a skirt.'

It was years ago he'd said that, and at the time it had hurt more deeply than she'd realised. Only when she'd come to terms with herself, had grown up somewhat, *and* when she'd finally realised that he really did find it attractive, had Helen got over the hurt.

Nowadays she merely dressed to minimise the effect, unconsciously choosing her clothes with a taste that was maturing as she did. Only when she wore a bikini did that aspect of her figure give her cause for concern.

'And in jeans,' she muttered, with a rueful grimace at the image in the mirror. She was now as slim as she'd ever been, thanks to the enforced diet of worry and being too often out of work, but in jeans she'd still appear broader in the beam than she preferred.

Tailored slacks? Not on the farm, Helen chuckled. It might be all very well in the movies, but she knew farm life as it really was, and jeans were the only practical garb. Especially in Tasmania, and more especially after nearly four years in sub-tropical Queensland.

She shivered at the thought, once again wondering if Dane had really been serious. Worse, what if he hadn't. That would leave her squarely behind the eight-ball again, with no home, no car, no money . . .

'Money!' She gasped out the word as realisation struck. How could he meet her at the plane? She didn't have enough money to get to the airport, much less fly to Hobart. Even to use her bank credit card would mean getting in deeper than she dared.

Her first impulse was to 'phone him back immediately, but she first had to find her diary with his telephone number in it. Then she thought better of 'phoning; having offered her a place to stay and something to keep her occupied, perhaps he'd be put out at being asked to pay the freight as well.

And suddenly, despite the recentness of their conversation, despite the warmth in his voice, the feelings he'd transmitted across the miles between them, Helen had second thoughts. How might he have changed, now that Vivian was gone? Did he really want her to come, or was he simply reacting to some half-felt obligation?

Maybe he did want her for a mistress. No, he would have said so, had that been the case, surely. During her younger years, neither he nor Vivian had spared bluntness when it came to helping her steer a course through life.

She could still remember the one night they'd all got stuck into the wine—herself, particularly—and trotted out their own moral standards for consideration. Not as an example, certainly not as something to be forced upon her or anyone else, but as a legitimate subject for discussion between adults.

She could still remember Dane saying: 'Virginity is a state of mind. Whether you have a sexual relationship with somebody isn't what's important; it's how you feel while you're about it. If it's the right thing to do for that time and that place and that person, great. But if it isn't . . . and you let yourself get pushed into something that cheapens you in your own estimation, then it's wrong.'

'But what about love?' she'd asked. 'And . . . and don't most men want their wives to be virgins?'

'In western society, I think only the insecure ones, whether they admit it or not,' Vivian had replied. 'Other societies, of course, are different, sometimes radically so.'

'And love is a state of mind, too,' Dane had continued. 'I love Vivian . . . I love you . . . hell, I love half a dozen women I could name, but that's quite different than whether I want to take them to bed. I could name another half a dozen I'd love to take to bed . . . once . . . but love them? Not on your life.'

Helen remembered looking at Vivian with horror at that statement. She was only twenty, then, and couldn't fathom the older woman's bland comprehension of such a statement. But Vivian had been smiling, a deep, fathomless smile of total security. And Dane had continued.

'I'll give you an analogy you should be easily able to understand,' he'd said. 'Visualise the farmer, driving to town in his battered old utility. He passes a car showroom, and there's this beautiful, low, slinky sports car sitting there. He stops for a look and the salesman asks if he'd like to take it for a drive. So he does. And he enjoys it immensely, but when the salesman starts trying to deal, what does the farmer say? "Not much good for my life-style, mate. Nice to drive it once, though."'

And he laughed at Helen's initial bewilderment and the sudden grin when the logic struck her.

'Now to me' ... and he named one of the more decorative ladies of their unanimous acquaintance ... 'is a sports car when what I need—and have—is a paddock ute.' And he'd laughed at Vivian's mock attempt to take offence at the analogy. But then he turned deadly serious in continuing.

'But for her sake, I just hope there's somebody out there who feels exactly the opposite, because if she never finds the man who's right for her, she'll go on being a sports car until her wheels fall off, and that would be a waste.'

And there was a sadness in his voice, then, that was mirrored in Helen's when she'd replied, 'But you'd still like to drive it—once?'

'If I didn't have more important things to do,' he'd replied, and she'd known, as Vivian had known, that he wasn't being evasive. He was stating a fact, as he saw it. His car-testing days were over. And he didn't really miss them, either.

'But where does that leave me?' she'd asked. 'Am I a ... a what? I can't really see myself as a Jaguar XKE, somehow.'

They'd all laughed at that, but it had been Dane who'd replied.

'When you're older, you'll be a damned fine family sedan,' he'd said. 'Correction, luxury family sedan. And probably a one-owner job.'

'Thank you ... I think,' she'd replied. And she had thought about it, later. Several times, usually under duress. What had surprised her most was how effective the word picture had become; it was very difficult indeed for an amorous young man to hustle her into bed when her mind was conjuring up visions of her wheels falling off.

But that was in the early years. Later, dating, she remembered, from her twenty-second birthday party, it

was another of Dane's comments that had kept her in
control when every aspect of her physical being urged
surrender. She would never forget the night for another
reason, either. It was when a man she thought was hers
became engaged to her best friend from school, and she
would have cried herself right out of the party but for
Dane saying, 'What the hell? You haven't lost a thing.
Listen, love. When you find somebody who loves you
as much as I do, then grab him, if you love him as
much back. But don't waste your time mucking about
with the tiddlers.'

And she'd taken a second look, from the safety of his
arms as they danced, and realised he was right. And
realised that she hadn't loved Peter, she'd only wanted
him, and she'd laughed in Dane's ear, 'He wasn't much
of a car anyway.'

'Underpowered, clutch slipping and bald tyres,' he'd
chuckled in reply, but it had been Vivian's sotto-voiced,
'definitely an economy model,' that had capped the
evening, driving away every cloud of despondency for
the rest of the evening.

Helen chuckled in glee as she wondered how Dane
would categorise Bryce. During their rare encounters
over the years since that birthday, she'd introduced him
to several eligible suitors without getting past the
economy car level. Except once, when they'd met
unexpectedly at a press club function in Canberra.

Helen had been escorted by a tall, dark, very
charming radio personality, a man Dane knew and . . .
she thought . . . liked. Fate had put them at the same
table, and the two men had been more than friendly
throughout the evening. She had been rapt, until . . .
leaving the table for the final dance of the evening,
she'd heard Dane mutter to Vivian, 'How'd we go,
driving the Birdsville Track in a 120Y?'

Her handsome escort's advances later that evening
had been stirring, but when it came to the crunch they
stirred only laughter at the mental image of his wheels

falling off. He hadn't asked her out again, and Helen wasn't overly sorry.

Pulling her mind back to the present, Helen laughed at the memory, then resumed her earlier search for the diary while cursing herself for being so disorganised.

She would have to call him back, she reasoned, even though the thought of having to borrow her fare was frankly repugnant. The fact that Dane would realise that didn't make it any better. Still, it wouldn't be the first time she'd borrowed money from him, always being scrupulous about repaying the loans on time.

'So at least my credit rating's okay, although having to 'phone long-distance—collect—to borrow money isn't my idea of the way to go about it. I wouldn't be surprised if he tells me to go jump,' she muttered to herself. 'And I wouldn't blame him if he did.'

She finally found her diary, in—as she might have expected—the absolute last place she would have thought to look, and was about to pick up the telephone when it began to ring.

Answering it, she sat in astonished silence as the airline representative explained that there was a direct flight from the Gold Coast to Hobart on Saturday, and that if it were suitable, she would find her tickets waiting when she arrived at the airport.

Helen thought, frantically, finally mumbled her acceptance and wrote down the necessary details, and when the conversation was over she sat staring numbly at the now silent telephone.

'Oh, Dane, you do think of everything,' she finally sighed, shaking her head as if that action could fling aside the tears that welled up to blur her vision.

It was half an hour before she could even begin to think of packing, and even longer before the threat of imminent tears had totally diminished.

CHAPTER TWO

THE plane journey was uneventful, especially in comparison to the chaotic days of preparation that preceded it. Days of packing and repacking, deciding what to take and what to throw out, days of final farewells to her few close friends in Brisbane and—very nearly at the last minute—to the girl whose flat Helen had been minding.

Lorna only arrived back from Europe on the Friday, and slept right through until the time when she had to rise to get Helen to the Gold Coast airport next day.

'Really, I think you're mad,' was her comment as they drove through the southern suburbs and into the crowded semi-rural zone that theoretically separated Brisbane from the Gold Coast.

'I don't see what's so mad about it,' Helen had replied, hardly bothering to argue now that the decision had been made.

'You will when you get off the plane and start freezing,' her friend replied. 'Or didn't you pay any attention to the weather on television last night? They've got snow down there, Helen . . . snow!'

And the words were uttered with the awe of a true Queenslander, believing that the Sunshine State was the centre of the universe and that snow, especially, was the devil's punishment on those fools who chose to live elsewhere. Lorna had never seen snow in her life before arriving in Europe six months earlier, and from the way she went on about it, Helen couldn't help feeling pity for any person to whom something that simple could remain the highlight of a six-month European tour.

It had been, in her own opinion, rather a wasted exercise for her friend, believing as Lorna did that even

27

the rest of Australia was somehow foreign territory. Europe had been as alien as Mars.

But from her own viewpoint, particularly at this point in time, Lorna's trip had proved a godsend. Unable to restrain herself in European shops, Lorna had arrived back with several tasteful woollen outfits that she'd never even worn and which, with hindsight had been no bargain at all, being quite unsuitable for Brisbane's temperate climate.

And as they were much of a size, Helen found that she had the bargains, paying give-away prices for clothing that she not only liked, but which was eminently suitable for the Tasmanian winter she was flying towards.

Deciding exactly what to wear for her journey had posed little difficulty, despite her certain knowledge that Dane might be waiting at the airport in anything from farm work clothes to evening wear.

'I might be a jillaroo, presuming they use the term in Tasmania, but I'm damned if I'll arrive looking like one,' she'd muttered to herself at one point. And had chosen for her trip a light woollen outfit in tones of beige and camel. The turtle-neck sweater was light enough to ensure comfort during the trip itself, and the matching jacket would ensure reasonable comfort once she had arrived in the southern capital.

Packed were her riding gear, several pairs of jeans and soft cotton shirts, the other good outfits she'd bought from Lorna and the few really good clothes she'd owned. Little enough, but during the past few years she'd come to realise that travelling lightly was the only sensible approach.

With her luck, she might get off the plane to find that Dane couldn't meet her as arranged, and she didn't fancy trying to manage half a dozen suitcases when one would do the job.

But that fear was nullified when she stepped from the aircraft and walked into the arrival terminal to a welcome that was all she might have wished for

Strong arms wrapped themselves around her and she felt the never-forgotten familiarity of a soft beard against her cheek as Dane growled, 'Welcome to paradise,' into her ear before enfolding her in an embrace she feared might crack her ribs.

She didn't really even get a chance to look at him until he'd set her down again and stood back, grinning hugely, his hands still imprisoning her waist.

It was, initially, confusing. He looked older, and yet somehow younger as well. There was a touch of grey in his hair now, but his face was tanned and his figure lean and fit. He moved with his old assurance, and now there was the addition of a tremendous physical vitality, due—she supposed—to his farm and the work involved.

She cocked her head slightly, looking up to meet his eyes and smiling her own welcome because she was so filled with warmth and happiness she hardly dared speak.

'You look marvellous for somebody who's on the breadline,' he grinned. 'You ought to give up eating more often; it agrees with you.'

A tribute to her maturing slenderness, only, but to Helen it was praise beyond price. 'You don't look so bad yourself,' she managed to reply.

'Considering my age and infirmities,' he replied. 'It must be all this good, clean living. I'm so fit, it's positively disgusting.'

And he looked it. Dressed in an expensive casual suit, with his shirt open at the neck to reveal a tanned, muscular throat, his entire being seemed to belie the grey in his hair and beard and the deep lines squinting from beside his deepset eyes.

Helen stepped free of his hands, striking an exaggerated pose as she deliberately surveyed him from top to toe, cocking her head first to one side and then the other.

'Yes, not too bad for an old man,' she finally said

with mock seriousness. 'I'll bet you cut quite a swath with the girls . . . about fifteen years ago.'

'Fifteen *minutes* ago,' he grinned. 'You should have seen what I had to leave in the airport bar to come collect you.'

'I'm surprised you bothered, then,' she replied, then paused, surprised at how tart the response sounded even in her own ears.

But Dane, not surprisingly, ignored or chose to ignore the acid in her reply. 'I hope they didn't feed you up too well on that flying sardine can,' he was saying, 'because I haven't eaten all day and one of the best restaurants in the entire country is only a few minutes from here.'

Helen, who'd easily turned away the airline's food, except for coffee *en route*, needed no persuading. They picked up her luggage when it arrived and within minutes were driving away in a large, luxuriously appointed station sedan.

In a tiny community which Dane explained was Cambridge, little more than an outer suburb of Hobart, they turned north on a narrow bitumen road and drove for about ten minutes to Richmond, which he said was the doyen of Tasmania's historic villages.

Prospect House, which had begun life as a sumptuous Georgian home in the 1830s, fairly took Helen's breath away. Nestled in an idyllic setting on the outskirts of the village, it fairly glowed with a newfound vitality as a licenced restaurant with its own private passport into history.

'Just as well I didn't arrive in my jodhpurs and riding boots,' she muttered as Dane handed her from the car. 'They'd have very likely made me eat on the back steps, or in the servants' quarters.'

He laughed, a full, rich sound that matched the welcome proffered by the elderly building.

'So long as you were clean and tidy, I doubt if anybody'd even notice,' he replied. 'Tasmanians—thank

God—don't seem to suffer the same ridiculous attitudes as the mainland. Much more relaxed, down-to-earth, sensible people. I still haven't figured out if it's the climate or the fact that tourism really is an important industry here, but I expect you'll find, as I have, that it's like living in another world.'

He followed her into the building, greeting the proprietor as an old friend, and quickly introduced Helen as 'another one with the good sense to get out of Queensland before they sell it to the Yankees.' He then explained that the proprietor and his wife had also come south from Queensland, albeit several years ago.

Helen found their friendly greetings tinged with something else, some faint, almost unidentifiable reserve, perhaps. And found herself wondering why, unless it was because—as he surely would have—Dane had brought Vivian here regularly before her death.

But no one else since? She wondered about that, debating if his grief at his wife's death was still so poignant, however well hidden, that he would have avoided their favourite restaurant with anyone else, or perhaps even entirely.

They sat over drinks while considering the extensive menu, which dazzled Helen with its choices. Squab in cream, Aramagnac and pâté sauce vied with salad of wood pigeon with black currant vinaigrette and roast venison, or hare casserole.

'About the only thing you won't find down here is the same approach to seafood,' Dane was saying. 'Oysters, I have to admit, aren't a patch on those in Queensland, and you sometimes don't see quite the standard of king prawns, but the scallops are ten times better and some of the deep-sea fish is phenomenal. This place, obviously, specialises in game, but if you're having adjustment problems I can recommend the yabbies to start with.'

She was tempted, but instead chose to begin with the quail and mushroom salad, tempted by the additions of chicory and pine nuts in a warm vinaigrette. And then the roast venison, because she'd never tasted venison in her life.

Dane, after insisting on an agreement that there'd be no trades allowed, selected the yabbies, and when the succulent little freshwater crayfish arrived before him, Helen could have kicked herself for so easily agreeing.

'You'll learn,' he chuckled, steadfastly refusing her even the smallest of tastes and continuing to be equally bloody minded when his squab arrived at the table.

Her own choices were so immensely pleasurable that she agreed to forgive him, provided a return visit might be arranged so she could try the rest of the menu.

'It'll depend on how well you behave,' he replied with a slow grin, then hoisted a glass of excellent wine and quite sombrely toasted her arrival. A gallant and pleasing touch, she thought, but hardly a patch on his next comment: 'And I'm glad you didn't arrive in your jodhpurs; what you're wearing is immensely more flattering.'

The simple sincerity of the compliment brushed away all chance of a flippant reply. She could only murmur her thanks and quickly looked down to her meal to hide the blush she feared was starting.

Damn the man, she thought. He could still charm the birds from the trees without even trying. And why shouldn't he? A swift calculation showed him still on the sunny side of forty by two years.

'You're only as old as you feel,' she thought, and didn't realise she'd spoken the thought until he grinned at her and replied.

'Well just don't get any funny ideas about feeling me to find out,' he chuckled. 'Old Mrs Buscombe wouldn't approve of such goings on in her very elegant home.'

At Helen's bemused look, he called over the host to explain that Mrs Buscombe was the wife of the house's builder, James Buscombe, in the 1830s. Her ghost, a friendly one, was reportedly seen by some visitors.

Helen was then given a brochure on Richmond, wherein she learned that another, later owner, had once shattered most of the windows while firing his cannon in the front garden during the 1860s.

'I'm glad he isn't still hanging round to haunt us,' she prompted. 'I think I'd much prefer a friendly old lady ... presuming I must have any sort of ghost at all.'

And couldn't help wondering if Mrs Buscombe were the only ghost present at Prospect House that evening. Was Vivian there too, lurking in their memories, a tangible spectre of Dane's grief? And if so, what would her reaction be to his too-flippant reply, or worse, to his blatant compliment and charm?

Helen shivered, telling herself silently that it was something she mustn't think of. There had been nothing between she and Dane during Vivian's lifetime to be ashamed of, and whatever might have been in her own *mind* on occasion was surely locked away too securely even for a ghost to discern.

Not that it mattered, really. Helen knew full well that Vivian had been quite aware of the crush she'd developed over Dane when he'd first stepped into her life. And had ignored it, secure in his love and the fact that a crush, if never returned, soon dies.

Only seeing him across the table now, Helen wasn't all that sure it had totally died. Perhaps put on the shelf would be a better description, although the unreturned aspect certainly still applied.

Then she shook herself mentally, glad that for the moment the two men were involved in a discussion that took their attention from her. What a thing to be thinking! And something she'd best *stop* thinking, now! If she were to start putting interpretations on Dane's kind invitation, it would only lead to problems, and she had quite enough of those without adding to them.

Whatever her own feelings, past, present or future, it would be an abuse of hospitality and plain bad manners to let her own imagination start reading things into the relationship that might not even exist.

They ended dinner with some of the most delightful desserts she'd ever seen created, then sat over coffee and port, both of them silent and staring into the open fire that kept the room so pleasantly warm. What thoughts lurked in Dane's mind at such a time, Helen wondered? Was he, perhaps, already regretting having invited her? Or thinking of Vivian and past meals here in this most marvellous of restaurants?

For her own part, she was comfortably replete, mildly sleepy from the excitement of the day overall, and rather wishing they could finish up and get home, wherever home was. From his infrequent letters she knew the farm was somewhere on the Huon, an area south of Hobart and bounded by the Huon River and the D'Entrecasteaux Channel leading to the mouth of the river Derwent, but how that related to their present position she hadn't a clue.

And I really should have, she thought idly. Imagine not even bothering to study a map when you're off to somewhere new. Slack, Helen, very slack!

Not that even a map would have helped much as they finally drove through darkness towards the lights of the city, then through the city centre itself on a maze of one-way streets before once again coming to rural travel as they headed, presumably, south.

Helen found herself dozing as Dane conveyed the vehicle smoothly along a route that seemed to be constantly either climbing or descending, twisting and turning as if the very land itself was on edge. But he drove with consummate skill, his entire concentration on the dark road before him, and she felt strangely safe and secure, much more so than if she'd been driving herself.

She was, in fact, so secure that she fell quite asleep before he finally turned into a narrow, gravelled driveway and stopped the vehicle. What woke her was

the deep-throated bark of a dog near at hand and
Dane's softly hissed, 'Quiet, Molly, that's a good girl.'

'Uhm ... do I have to get up?' Helen sighed, still
only half-aware of what was happening.

'Unless you fancy sleeping in the car and probably
freezing off some valuable part of your anatomy,' was
the reply, coupled with the opening of the car door to
introduce a chilling breeze that brought her instantly
awake.

'I'll pass, thank you,' she gasped, and scurried to
follow as he disembarked and hurried to grab up her
luggage from the rear.

She could see the house only vaguely in the dim
moonlight, and her first impression was of sprawling,
long-established permanence. When Dane snapped on a
light to show the way down a long footpath to the gate,
she got a glimpse of white weatherboards beneath a
shroud of vines with carefully-tended flower-beds at
their feet.

At the gate, a leaping black shape revealed itself to be
a Labrador bitch who quieted instantly at a word from
her master, but kept Helen under a watchful, apparently
resentful, stare.

'I don't think she likes me,' Helen murmured as Dane
flung open the gate, and was immediately proved wrong
as the dog pranced up to lick at her fingers and give a
little wriggle of pleasure as Helen stooped to scratch her
behind the ears.

'She likes everybody,' he replied casually. 'And
besides, I've taught her she's not to bite the pretty girls
... only the ugly ones. Now let's get inside before we all
freeze to death.'

Helen followed through a long, narrow porch filled
with dog leashes, gumboots and work clothing, past a
neat stack of stove wood, and into a rambling farm
kitchen that was comfortably warm compared to the
chill outside.

Then, through a series of passages to a small, tidy

room with a three-quarter bed, wardrobe, walls full of
bookshelves and a door that appeared to lead to an
adjoining bathroom. On the bed, a fluffy, down-filled
quilt promised warm sleeping, and on the floor beside
the bed sat a pair of obviously new sheepskin slippers.

'You'll need those around here,' Dane muttered,
following her glance. 'Get into them after you've
freshened up, then come on out for a nightcap and I'll
show you the rest of the house.'

Even with the small radiant heater he'd thoughtfully
provided, Helen found the room icy, and she was glad
enough, having changed to jeans and a warm
sweatshirt, to join him in the warmth of the kitchen
where a large cast-iron stove threw a pleasant glow into
the room.

Molly rose from where she'd been sprawled in front
of the fire, but after a gentle nuzzle at Helen's fingers,
promptly returned to flop down again in the warmth.

Dane had also changed, and now looked quite in
place with his surroundings. A soft flannel shirt, sleeves
rolled halfway to his elbows, hung loosely over faded,
well-worn jeans, and his feet, like hers, were encased in
soft sheepskin boots.

'It'll take a bit before this room's warmed up
properly,' he said with a slow grin. 'Fancy a small
brandy to carry along while I give you the two-dollar
tour?'

'Whatever you're having,' she replied, then looked
away as it suddenly dawned on her that he looked more
than just fit ... he was intensely, almost startlingly
masculine in these casual clothes, an effect enhanced by
his lithe, easy way of moving, the obvious strength of
his muscular body.

It seemed as if the polish she'd seen on the man
she'd first met had been only a veneer, almost a
disguise of the person inside. This, she realised, was
the true Dane Curtis. A man equally at home in the
crowds of the city streets or in the bush, but much

more at ease where he now stood, in his own home, on his own land.

His smile hadn't changed, nor had his charm. But his eyes had; they were clearer, somehow more astute. He looked down at her as he handed across her drink, and his gaze was blatantly appraising, not really in a sexual fashion, and not meant to make her uncomfortable despite how easily he saw past her own veneer to the vulnerable person beneath.

'Bit late to be wondering if you ought to have come, isn't it?' he asked with startling accuracy.

Helen breathed in deeply before replying, half-tempted to stall by sipping at her drink, then wondering why she should suddenly have such trepidations in the first place.

'I was more wondering why *you* thought I ought to come,' she finally replied, ordering up boldness to cover the quiver inside. 'There has to be more to it than just giving me chance to get my head together.'

'Why?' It was a blunt, direct question, but asked softly, so softly she barely heard it.

'You were pretty firm about getting me to stand on my own feet a few years ago,' she replied with equal softness. 'And things have been a lot more desperate, once or twice, since then. So why drag me back now? I think it's out of character.'

He chuckled, the sound low and rumbling in his muscular throat. But he had no trouble meeting her eyes.

'You're getting awful suspicious and cynical for someone so young,' he replied. 'I warned you that would happen if you stayed in journalism.'

'You warned me it had *better* happen if I was going to stay in journalism,' she corrected without heat in her reply. 'So don't complain when—for once, anyway—I've followed your advice.'

'About time.'

'There've been other times.' And she wondered what

in hell they were doing, sparring like this. But then, what should she expect? She'd not seen him in two years, hadn't written as regularly or informatively as she should. And how could he be the same ... with the death of a woman he'd loved so deeply, the total change in life-style, the probable loneliness.

Loneliness! That would account for much, she thought. Oddly enough, she hadn't even thought of the effect loneliness might have on a man she'd always thought of as something of a loner. But he hadn't been, not really. He'd always had Vivian, until her death. But now ... how difficult it must have been for him since she'd gone.

Her own loneliness over the past few years had been quite different, created as it was by the self-imposed conditions of her career. And she was younger, less rigidly set in her ways.

Helen looked at him, words of sympathy forming on the tip of her tongue like dew on a flower petal, but the words remained unspoken, because he got in first.

'Well I'm just glad you took my advice this time,' he said, stepping forward to gather her into his arms, adding, 'Welcome,' as he pulled her against him, tucking her head neatly in against the firm, warm pulse of his throat as he held her close.

Helen's own arms flung themselves around his neck as the pot of her scalding tears boiled over, and for long moments they stood entwined in silence before she finally looked up through blurred eyes, offering her mouth not as a woman but as a child in need of that final phase of comforting.

And he kissed her with the infinite gentleness her offering demanded ... at first. Then she could feel the held-in sexuality as her own response began to change, as her body began to react to the closeness of his own, her nipples thrusting against his chest, her bones turning to liquid rubber as her lips began searching for a new response, her femininity crying out to him silently and yet ever so loudly.

For one, tiny instant, she felt his fingers begin a score of paradisaical music along the keyboard of her spine, felt their bodies begin to flow together, but then his hands slid quickly to her waist, his lips releasing themselves. Gently, but oh, so damned firmly.

And there was a resounding smack as the palm of his hand connected with her bottom, completing the separation process with that single gesture. And when his voice came, it was still gentle, still loving, but also filled with a no-nonsense aura she'd come to recognise when working with him.

'You're getting too big for this sort of thing. From now on you can wash your own damned back,' he muttered, both admitting and denying their united response in the same breath. And, more important, levying his demand for her acceptance of his decision without denying his difficulty in making it.

'But who's going to wash yours?' she managed to reply, voice unnaturally light, her eyes turned away to hide her tears as much as to keep her from seeing what glint of embarrassment might lurk in his own. Flippancy was her only recourse, and they both knew and accepted that.

'Mine? Hell, there's a list a mile long,' he growled in reply. 'I've got to beat them away with a bloody great stick, you ought to know that.'

Dane, too, taking refuge in being flippant. Typically, she thought. Too inherently honest to deny what they'd both felt, what they both understood could have happened, but also too strong to have let it happen. And she? Was she also so strong? That question was best ignored entirely.

'Oh, but of course,' she replied with a false grin, adding an emphatic shake of her head for good measure. 'So that's why you invited me . . . to help you make a choice. So what's the strategy—are you going to trot up a new one every day for vetting . . . or what?'

'Well I did think you ought to have a few days' rest

first,' he replied, now striding over to pick up his drink again and yet still not quite meeting her eyes. Helen, for her part, was glad to pick up her barely tasted brandy, needing the fieriness of it to burn the taste of him from her lips.

Given these few seconds of retrospect, she realised the danger of that impromptu intimacy, recognising almost instinctively his contrary need to show her he cared and yet to keep her at arm's length just because he did care.

'Oh, you can start tomorrow, for all of me,' she grinned, throwing herself into the word-game whole-heartedly because in no other way could she remove the strain from both of them. 'I'm young and tough ... a bit of flying doesn't knock too much out of me. I can take it.'

'Maybe. But I sure as hell couldn't,' he replied with a matching grin. 'Now come look at the rest of the place, so you'll be able to find your way round in the morning.'

Afterwards, lying alone in the room where she suddenly felt terribly, terribly alone, Helen realised that her only real impression during the short tour of the house was how much of Vivian remained.

Obviously, he either hadn't bothered or hadn't wanted to change things around; there were the same pictures, the same ornaments, the furniture layout was Vivian's beyond doubt. Newer, different furniture, mostly, than she remembered from other places they'd lived. Solid, heavy pieces designed for comfort as well as style.

The house, obviously, was very old and had been somewhat neglected before they'd bought the farm, Dane told her. He was still unsure if it was worth restoring, or if he should someday pull it down and replace it.

'It's got no historic value or anything, except that it's at least twice as old as I am,' he'd said. 'And when things go wrong—as they seem to quite regularly—my first instinct is to throw a match at it and start fresh. But on the good days, well, it's got something. Personality, character ... something. When you come right down to it, there's only the kitchen that's really bad, and wrongly located as well. So maybe someday I'll put on an extension to shift the kitchen and modernise it.'

Helen couldn't help but agree with his assessment of the kitchen, which was laid out, it seemed, for maximum inconvenience and inefficiency. Useable, certainly, but she shuddered to imagine earlier residents trying to feed large families from such a kitchen. Cooking for one or two wouldn't have been too bad, but she wondered at Vivian's reaction the first time she'd got involved in one of her almost-famous dinner party productions. Vivian would have hated that kitchen after a week, and yet ... she'd been using it nearly a year when she'd been killed. Helen wondered, then, why they'd done nothing to fix the problems.

Sleep was very difficult, at first. She lay there, only just warm enough, trying to turn off her mind. It had been a long day, a day filled with minor tensions and excitements, but nothing, Helen thought to herself, that should make getting to sleep so terribly difficult.

And suddenly, she knew what it was ... or wasn't! It was the silence. She had heard Dane step outside to kennel the dog, heard him return to the house, stoke the fire for the night, and retire to his own bedroom. But since then ... nothing! It was an almost tangible silence, lacking as it did the traffic noises, the people noises that never quite stopped in the city.

And so dark. Without the street lights, the passing vehicles, and since the night was moonless, the darkness outside her window was total. It was like peering into an ink bottle.

Then memory took over, dragging her back to her childhood on the land, and memories of similar dark nights, similar still, quiet times, the feeling of being quite alone in the entire world, snug and warm and where nothing could intrude.

Moments later, she was asleep, sunk into a warm, dreamless nothingness that lasted through until the first glimmerings of pickaninny dawn. But it wasn't the dawn that woke her, much less having had sufficient sleep. And it was no gentle, slow awakening.

What brought her leaping from the bed with a squeal of terror to plunge wide-eyed and terrified through the house was a moaning, gasping, choking cry of such anguish, such torment, that it seemed to continue ringing in her ears even as she lurched into the kitchen to find—astonishingly—Dane sitting calmly at the table, a cup of coffee before him and one dark eyebrow raised enquiringly at her sudden, dramatic entrance.

But before either of them could speak, she heard it yet again, and could only point in mute silence towards the sound's direction.

Even as she did so, Helen realised that this time the sound was slightly different, further away. And while the first had been like a foghorn being tortured to death, this second moaning wail had overtones of a million rusty gate hinges being manipulated in unison. And Dane didn't seem to hear them at all!

'I'd have saved you a cup, you know? There was no need to come flying out as if the devil was after you,' he grinned, gesturing Helen towards an empty chair and rising to pour coffee into a second cup already waiting. 'White with two sugar, if I remember right . . .?'

'My God! Are you deaf!' The words burst forth, followed quickly by more, words that were gasped into existence by the fright Helen felt. 'You must be deaf . . . or else I'm going mad. Something's dying out there. Dying horribly. I heard it right outside the window and you're just . . . just sitting there. You must have heard it . . . you must have!'

'Settle down . . . settle down,' he said, putting the

coffee before her with one hand and using the other to steady her, much as one might calm a frightened colt. And she looked up to see a strange, almost unholy laughter lurking in his eyes, a laughter that fought against the bonds which held it until it could burst free, exploding in a convulsive torrent that had him writhing in his own chair, tears streaming down his cheeks.

And every time he looked at her, seeing the confusion she felt, reading the growing uncertainty in her eyes, hearing the stuttered questions that died half-formed, unable to match the totality of his laughter, it seemed to get worse.

'I'm sorry,' he finally managed to gasp. 'It's just that—oh, hell, you'd better come see for yourself. I can't explain it, or at least I won't, save to say that it doesn't bode well for your career as a jillaroo, dear Helen.'

'And I don't think we can be thinking of the same thing,' she retorted, half angry now. 'Dane . . . Didn't you *hear* it?'

'Well of course I did, and so did you. The only difference is that I know what we heard and you, dear girl, obviously don't. And, I suppose, it woke you out of a sound sleep. Oh dear, oh dear, I shouldn't laugh, really I shouldn't. You're going to have my guts for garters when I show you!'

And he was leading her, half-dragging her along as he strode off through the house, not pausing until he reached the door of Helen's room. There, he paused.

'You go look. Just go over and look out the window. I won't come, because I want some running room in case you decide to do something that makes me sound like that,' he said, and gently shoved her through the half-open door.

His chuckles echoed in her ears as Helen walked determinedly over to pull aside the curtains, staring out into the mid-dawn light with a mixture of fear and curiosity. And then with sheer astonishment as her eyes met—not fifteen feet away—two huge, placid, blue-brown eyes that solemnly stared back at her. Warm, friendly eyes, a soft, pliable muzzle and two great long ears that seemed to wave a greeting at her.

Helen was dumbstruck. She could only stand there, returning the large donkey's patient stare and watching in silence as it wrinkled its lips to bray out yet another blood-curdling, yodelling command that was immediately answered from somewhere in the distance, out of her sight.

A donkey. A big, big donkey, probably thirteen hands high. And a fair age, if her horse experience was anything to go by. Helen had seen donkeys before, but she'd certainly never heard one, much less right outside her bedroom window bellowing her out of a sound sleep. No wonder Dane had laughed, but it was . . . not . . . funny! Not one damned bit funny, she decided.

Dane was sitting, nursing his coffee with apparent calm, when she marched back to the kitchen and stood just inside the door, glaring at him.

'You . . . you bastard!' she hissed. 'You dirty, rotten, scheming, underhanded . . . You might have warned me, at least.'

'About what? How the hell was I supposed to know——' And he couldn't go on. The laughter broke him up again, erupting in such infectious hysteria that her anger retreated before it, could do nothing else. Seconds later she, too, was laughing, realising how funny it was—in retrospect.

'How . . . how many of them have you got?' she was finally able to ask, some long moments later and with half a cup of coffee inside her.

'Four. You'll meet them all when we go to do the morning feeding, which is rather overdue. That's partly why Maria's carrying on, apart from the fact I'm weaning her baby and she's feeling all lonely and neglected. And really Helen . . .' with a chuckle '. . . I'm sorry she woke you up. But if I'd set one foot outside

the door, you'd have been wakened anyway, as you'll
see when we go.'

And she did! Having quickly thrown on some jeans
and a sweatshirt, then one of Dane's jackets and a pair
of gumboots, she followed him out into the morning
sunshine and a cacophony of sound that *certainly*
would have wakened her . . . it would have wakened the
dead, she thought.

They were no sooner out the door when Molly
barked a greeting and thundered madly around in her
kennel, demanding her freedom. A half-dozen huge
geese, stridently demanding attention, arrived from
somewhere to yammer at the garden gate, then several
ducks joined in, some of them flying from a pond in
the next paddock. An old nanny goat, baaing
impatiently, thrust her way into the flock, followed by a
black-faced lamb with an even more insistent wail.

From a long, low structure beside the barn, she could
hear the excited snuffling and grunting of several pigs,
and a variety of cackling chickens streamed in from
various directions.

She and Dane walked to the barn surrounded by his
menagerie, each one of them demanding food and
attention and determined to be first in line. And as they
approached the barn, several other goats and three
donkeys lined up at the fence like spectators at a
sporting match.

'I don't believe this,' she cried, struggling in her over-
sized gumboots to keep her footing amidst the horde of
noisy, pushy animals. 'What are you . . . old McDonald
reincarnated?'

'Sometimes I wonder,' he grinned. 'I really do.' But
he didn't, Helen realised. He didn't wonder at all. He
was so obviously enjoying himself that it was a pleasure
to watch.

And then to help. As she reached the barn he was
already handing out a container filled with chook
pellets and directions for her to go fling them 'over

there . . . so we get some of this lot out of the way for a minute, anyway.'

And then he was battling to get into the various stock food bins while at the same time keeping the old goat and the lamb from joining him inside the barn. A moment later, they were busy and eye-deep in buckets of feed, and Dane was striding off towards the piggery, Molly prancing happily beside him.

Helen stood and watched as he ladled out feed, refilled water troughs and did the required other chores, then followed as he walked over to fling some hay across to where the other goats and the three donkeys waited patiently for their share.

Only then did she realise that somehow, miraculously, the noise had all stopped. There wasn't a bleat or a cackle or a grunt or a squeal anywhere.

'Now that we can hear ourselves think,' Dane said, 'come and meet the rest of the crew.' And he solemnly introduced her to Mistral, Maria's foal, 'Nine months old and look at the size of him. He's going to be a good, big boy, this one,' and Joshua, a chocolate gelding with cream-coloured muzzle and appealing, spectacle rings around both eyes, and his sister, a tidy, blue-grey donkey named Trumpet the Strumpet.

'Which she is,' he muttered. 'That animal has every bad, stereotyped habit that's ever been labelled feminine . . . and more.'

'I think she's lovely,' Helen replied, ignoring the fact that her instinctive preference was for the chocolate gelding with his spectacled, friendly eyes and calm manner. Trumpet was distinctly flighty, although it wasn't much wonder, considering Dane's explanation that neither was even halter-broken, yet.

They stopped on the way back to the house for a visit to Maria, and Helen immediately decided she liked the old girl best of all. Maria, she was told, had been captured from a wild herd in central Australia many years before, and apart from an inclination to stubbornness, had few real faults.

'She rules the rest of them with an iron hand ... or rather hoof,' Dane said. 'Marches around so haughty you wouldn't believe it, like the chairwoman of a posh, ritzy women's club.'

It wasn't until they were back in the kitchen that his curious reticence during that telephone conversation sprang to mind, and his promise, and the one animal they hadn't met during morning rounds. Helen already thought she knew the answer, but still she had to ask, just to stir him a bit.

And she wasn't at all surprised when she asked, 'Where's my horse?'

She got the half-expected reply, 'What horse? I never promised you a horse.'

CHAPTER THREE

'YOU are a cunning, devious, sneaky so-and-so,' Helen said accusingly, but her heart wasn't in it. She'd been had, and they both knew it, but she'd done it all herself.

Dane only grinned. 'Shall I quote?' he said. And without waiting for a reply, he continued, 'I want something to ride. Doesn't have to be a flash Arabian or anything, but something at least fit to throw a saddle on.'

'Which shows it's not much wonder I'm out of a job,' Helen sighed. 'Talk about not checking my facts ... well ...'

'Your trouble is, you're just too damned innocent,' he replied with another grin. 'You just wander around all day with your mouth open, waiting for a new chance to stick your foot in it.'

'That isn't fair!' Helen cried. 'I mean ... surely to God I should be able to trust *you*!'

'Me least of all,' was the reply, and there was a grimness in his voice, a faint, almost imperceptible warning, but she couldn't quite tell if it was directed at her, or himself.

'I'll certainly keep that in mind,' Helen retorted, rising to pour each of them a third cup of coffee. She shouldn't, and knew it; she'd be hyper all day. But Dane had such a dastardly ability to get her stirred up and keep her there that she needed something to do with her hands. And if nothing else, she determined, she could always throw it at him.

'Well then stop trying to force yourself to be shirty,' he said. 'Actually you'll probably enjoy riding Maria. She hasn't got a vicious bone in her body, but she's a cunning old devil, and you've got to be on guard constantly that she doesn't just happen to find a convenient tree or fence post to rub you off against, or a low branch to walk under, or whatever. She needs somebody with a bit of experience to take her in hand.'

'Experience? I've never ridden a donkey in my entire life,' Helen snapped.

Dane, however, seemed impervious to her reaction. 'Well it's not a helluva lot different than riding a horse, is it?' he replied. 'And besides, nobody says you have to ride a donkey. Nobody's saying you have to do anything! You're here to have a holiday . . . a rest . . . a change of scene. You can do absolutely nothing but sit and contemplate your navel for the next month, if that's what makes you happy.'

'But you'd rather I spent my time riding Maria and working with the others so they're manageable,' Helen replied, not making it a direct question as much as thinking out loud.

'I would rather you did whatever makes you happy,' Dane replied firmly. 'But it isn't up to me to make that decision. You ought to know me well enough by now to realise that I'm not interested in running your life for you, Helen. I've got quite enough to do with running my own, thank you.'

Simple. Perhaps too simple. And yet why was she being so damned suspicious in the first place. Helen wondered. Dane, of all people, she ought to be able to trust, disregarding his own opinion on that exact question. But . . .

'Do you honestly expect me to believe that my experience with horses had nothing to do—nothing at all—with your invitation?' she demanded.

'Of course it had something to do with it,' was the rather unexpected reply. But he wasn't upset by her suspicions, nor rattled by the tone of her comments. Dane replied almost too calmly. 'But only in the sense that I reckoned the donkeys might give you something to do if you were threatened with boredom.'

'And does that mean you expect me to get bored?' Helen couldn't help asking that question, unfair as she realised it might sound.

'I don't honestly know what I expected, in that regard,' he replied, eyes regarding her soberly. 'For myself, the thing I like best about being out here is that I never have much chance to be bored, but there's no hard-and-fast rule says you have to feel the same. I suppose it's just something we'll have to wait and see.'

He paused long enough to slurp down the remainder of his coffee, then continued before Helen could think of a reply. 'Or rather, you can wait and see. I'm off to hibernate in my office until lunch, which means there's a great big do-not-disturb sign on the door except in vital emergencies.'

And he was halfway out of the room before she could stop him with a cry of, 'But wait! Who's going to make lunch? Me? And if so . . . what do you want to eat?'

Dane paused only long enough to grin at her. 'Don't hassle so much. We can organise lunch when it's time for lunch . . . and without getting all in a tizz about it. See you at twelve.'

Leaving her standing there, Helen decided, very much like a child who's been told to go off and play, to amuse herself without disturbing the adults.

Which was, she also decided, almost annoying. Certainly distracting. Although Dane, obviously, wasn't at all distracted; she heard his typewriter begin to chatter almost as soon as the office door had closed behind him.

Not totally sure if she was being patronised or what, she spent a few minutes cleaning up the coffee cups, another few unpacking clothes and arranging her room, and then . . . then what, she wondered. Torn between the desire to go outside and inspect the menagerie at her leisure or just relax with a good book, Helen glanced out at a glowering sky and decided on the latter. Besides, tizz or no tizz, she was determined that *she* would prepare lunch.

The difficulty was in deciding what to prepare. She knew Dane hadn't had breakfast, discounting the coffee, but she was sure that he seldom did. But whether or not he ate a big lunch, or just something light, she had no idea. She didn't usually eat breakfast herself, nor much for lunch as a general rule, but now she felt the need for something substantial, either because of sheer nervous reaction or because of the definite change in climate.

A check in the refrigerator revealed several pork chops, sufficient left-over boiled potatoes for a decent serving of hash-browns, and just enough salad fixings to get by with.

But it was nowhere near time to start the preparations, so she returned to her book, wondering if she dared interrupt him to offer morning coffee. Then decided against it. If he felt like coffee, he'd come out and organise it; the verbal do-not-disturb sign applied to her as much as anyone.

Dane didn't, in fact, emerge from his office until a few minutes before noon, and when he did venture forth he looked quite distinctly pleased with himself. Then he looked at the table set for lunch, the pork chops sizzling merrily in the frying pan, and his focus of pleasure shifted directly to Helen.

'I knew I shouldn't have invited you down here; you're already starting out to spoil me rotten,' he smiled. And sat down to his lunch with an enthusiasm that more than matched her own impatient hunger.

'Well,' he said when the meal was done and they had both leaned back to enjoy a cigarette and their coffee, 'it's a good thing I had such a productive morning, because I'll have to go do some physical work now, to wear all that away in time for dinner. And, of course, retract my criticisms of your cooking, if that's any example.'

'Thank you, I think,' Helen replied with a shy grin. 'But I think you'd best reserve judgment. I might have been lucky.'

'Well you'd best watch out, or you'll find yourself lumbered with it on a regular basis, but all right, I'll reserve judgment for a bit. At least until I've seen whether you can handle one of our big, home-grown ducks and a proper roast of pork. Stuff up either of those and I'll be forced to marry you off to somebody with less discerning a palate than mine.'

Helen couldn't help but laugh, despite the implied compliment. 'Your problem really *is* having been spoiled rotten,' she replied. 'And remembering Vivian's cooking, I'm not surprised...' Then she stopped, suddenly, wondering if she ought to have mentioned that.

Was Dane still sensitive to the point that he'd rather not be reminded of his wife? Not surprising, if true; they'd been as close as any couple Helen had ever met, and far closer than most.

But he merely grinned at her, a grin of total reassurance even before he spoke. 'No, love, you're not going to have to run around worrying about things like that. I'm sensitive, but I'm not paranoid, and I'm not carrying around any ghosts in my pockets. Viv was ... unique. And you know the way I felt about her. But she's gone, and sorry as I am for that, I know all any of us can do is remember her with love and ... well, you know what I mean.'

'Yes, I think so,' Helen replied. 'But still, I don't envy the next woman in your life, presuming, of course, that there is one. Vivian would be a terribly hard act to follow.'

'What makes you think there isn't one already?' he asked, and laughed as Helen's eyes widened with surprise. Then he continued before she could say a word.

'Hah! That got you, didn't it? But more seriously, if the *right* woman had been standing at the graveside, I'd have taken her home with me, and Viv would have cheered all the way from wherever she is now, just as

I'd have done if the circumstances had been reversed. And you think that's a horrible thing to say, don't you, Helen?'

'I think you're exaggerating just a bit,' Helen replied cautiously. 'Especially as I know very well that no other woman even *existed* for you while Vivian was alive, despite all the smart remarks you used to make about window-shopping. And she knew it too, so don't bother to try and deny it.'

'So . . .?' He was fishing, now, but for what? Helen waited, but it seemed that was to be Dane's only reaction. He was waiting for her to continue. And then he wasn't.

'But I suppose what you're trying to say is that because Vivian loved you, she'd want you to remarry or . . . whatever, and certainly not to spend the rest of your life mourning,' Helen finally said.

'And she also wouldn't want me putting some poor girl in the invidious position of having to feel she was Viv's *successor*,' Dane replied, a note of bitterness creeping in. 'God, what a cruel thing to do to anybody under the pretext of love. And done, as you very well know, far too often.'

True, Helen thought. They both knew people who'd remarried, only to spend their time drawing comparisons, usually unfair ones. How, she wondered, could anyone love somebody and persist in putting them as second-best? But then, how could anyone allow themselves to be placed in such a position . . . except if they were in love?

'All right,' she finally said. 'I understand what you mean, I suppose. But how can you *not* make comparisons? It must be inevitable, especially when . . . well think about it. I haven't even seen you in two years, but I cook one meal and I have to make a comparison. It's . . . it's human nature.'

'It's stupidity, that's what it is,' he growled, and there was real anger behind that growl, though she sensed he was deliberately controlling it, stage-managing it to perfection.

'It's not!' Helen denied. 'It's perfectly normal reaction. Especially when you're dealing with a known quantity. Lord, I'll never forget the first time I ever had you both over to dinner; I was terrified, absolutely terrified. Because I knew how good a cook Vivian was, and how good a cook I wasn't——'

'And you turned out a rather splendid leg of lamb, as I remember,' Dane interrupted. 'Especially so, considering you're the girl who always said you hated lamb, after having been raised on it and because of the God-awful way your mother used to cook it. We were both quite proud of you, as I remember, although of course you couldn't quite understand why.'

'And I'm a much better cook now,' Helen said. 'But I'm not in Vivian's class and very likely never will be.'

'So what?' was the brusque reply. 'You could be the best in the world, but if you had to compete with a ghost you'd lose. Nobody can compete with a memory, and nobody but a monster would expect them to.'

'Yes but——'

'Yes but what?' And now the anger wasn't stage-managed. Now she could see it gleaming hotly from his eyes, see it in the stern set of his jaw and feel it in the ragged timbre of his voice. 'I suppose next you'll be telling me that you could quite understand it if I occasionally allowed myself to make comparisons, and *you* probably could, because you're a very tolerant, understanding person on your better days. So I am telling you now . . . no comparisons. None! Is that quite clear?'

'Yessir! Anything you say, sir! Of course, sir!' Helen snapped out her retorts to cover the confusion and hurt she felt. Why was he being so touchy? So . . . so distinctly aggressive? She felt her eyes dissolving, started to rise, to flee to the safety of her room, only to run into a wall that closed softly and firmly around her, holding her gently.

'Poor girl,' a soft voice crooned in her ear. 'I bring you down here for a rest and immediately start rousting the hell out of you. But Helen ... that's the whole problem. You're here to sort out who *you* are, and throwing yourself into competition with a memory isn't the way to do it.'

'I know who I am!' The violence of her reply shook her, even to the point where she thrust herself from his arms, fire blazing in her soft eyes, burning off the tears. 'I *know* who I am! And I'm not trying to compete with anybody. That's not what I'm here for, remember? I'm here to be a sort of jillaroo ... the Dane Curtis cure for unemployment. And that's all!'

'And just see that you remember it,' he replied, scowl turning to something that might have been a grin. 'Yes, young Helen, I certainly shall. Indeed.'

'Well see that you do,' she retorted. 'And please don't call me *young* Helen. I am, in case you've forgotten, all of twenty-five years old, I'm no longer a child.'

'Yes,' he said, 'I'm beginning to see that, I think.' And before she could move his arms had closed around her once again, without that incredible gentleness, this time, pulling her tight against him as his lips dipped to claim her own. His kiss was fierce, demanding, almost punishing, his lips crushing hers as his hands pulled her tighter to him, hip to hip, her breasts crushed against his chest, her thighs all too aware of the hard muscle against them.

This was no brotherly kiss, held no hint of chaste affection. It was demanding, demanding of a response her body couldn't deny, didn't even think of denying. The heat rushed up from somewhere inside her, melting her bones, softening her lips as they moulded to his. The tide of her desire was like an electric shock; the realisation of *his* was a lightning bolt.

And dispersed as if by a lightning rod within seconds. Dane stopped kissing her as quickly as he'd begun, stepping away to stand looking down into her eyes with a look that held both passion and gentleness, shock and awareness. But mostly rejection.

'Well I don't think we'll try that again, Helen,' he said, and it was almost with a sigh, although Helen didn't somehow think it would have been a sigh of disappointment. 'Nor, shall we discuss emotion-laden subjects again, at least not for a day or so. I doubt my old system would stand it,' he continued. 'No, I think I shall whip through these dishes and then see about walking off that most excellent lunch. You may come, but only if you promise not to talk.'

Helen nodded mutely, hardly trusting herself to speak. How could she? Inside her, the molten flow of passion was only barely starting to cool, chilled—but not quickly—by the fierceness of her wanting, by the sheer physical need that her body had so abruptly exhibited. By the realisation that she could never think of Dane Curtis as an elder brother figure, not ever again.

She was shaken. She had been able to handle her crush on him, now seemingly a lifetime ago, because of the understanding attitude both he and Vivian had taken towards it. And because it had been just a crush, a childish thing relatively easily outgrown.

But this ... this sudden onslaught of a desire so vivid, so all-encompassing. So ... physical. It frightened her, and as they stood side by side at the sink, she realised it must also have frightened Dane. Certainly it had shaken him; and there could be no denying that his physical reaction had very nearly matched her own.

Worst of all, however, was that now something was changed in their relationship. Something vital and yet ... so difficult to put into words without cheapening it.

The dishes were done in an uncomfortable silence, a silence that continued when they'd put on boots and jackets, gathered up Molly, and strolled off through the paddocks with a retinue of donkeys and goats.

Dane seemed relatively untroubled, although deep in

thoughts that Helen thought she could guess with some accuracy. For her own part, she *was* troubled, because something in that one kiss and the reactions to it had lurched her into a loneliness she knew would not have otherwise existed. Before, he might have taken her hand, might have at least smiled to show that yes he was with her and yes, he cared. But now, they might as well have been strangers, and the feeling made her more lonely than if she'd stayed in Queensland.

The long, silent stroll didn't really accomplish much, and when they returned Dane buried himself in his office for another two hours before emerging to go feed the livestock. As she'd done in the morning, Helen joined him, making mental note of the quantities and the routine involved.

But it wasn't until dinner that night that the air was cleared, or at least cleared as much as it could be. Dane began it.

'I have to say I'm sorry for over-reacting this afternoon,' he said. Without preamble. Without any warning at all to help Helen prepare herself for the conversation.

'You don't *have* to say it,' she eventually replied, the words dropping into the silence like rocks into a deep pool. 'I . . . I think I understand.' A lie, or at least partly a lie, because she really didn't understand all of it. Least of all, perhaps, her own reactions. But she did understand the need for his attempt at an apology.

'Good.' And it was as if he'd stop there, except he added, astonishingly, 'And I'm glad to see you realise it's mostly your own fault.'

'*My* fault?' The question emerged more as a squeal of indignation and outrage, then disintegrated into a fumbling, mixed-up torrent of words that made no sense at all. And then into laughter as she saw the mocking gleam in his eye and realised that he'd deliberately made the comment just to break the tension.

'All right, Dane,' she managed to chuckle. 'I suppose I should have realised you wouldn't be able to handle all this pulchritude, so I'll take the blame. And to make it up to you—provided you're good, of course—I'll even see about spending some time breaking your damned donkeys.'

Then she grinned, a wicked grin, she hoped. 'To harness, since obviously you're too old and infirm to be riding. I think a nice little cart with red wheels would be appropriate, with a special rack for your canes.'

And they both laughed, secure now in the knowledge that the tension had been destroyed, and that although neither might be able to forget the incident earlier in the day, at least it had been defused.

Certainly, Helen realised when she was alone in her bed, she wouldn't soon forget it. Nor did she really want to, not until she'd more fully savoured the potential pleasures of it.

Huddled beneath her eiderdown, secure in the dark stillness of the room, she found herself reliving the taste of his kiss, the touch of him against her, her own frenzied stirring of emotion, of physical desire. It was, she decided, almost wicked to have enjoyed anything quite that much. Especially when it meant that someone she cared for was troubled by the circumstances.

That, of course, was the problem. Much as the demon inside her revelled in the thought that Dane might now be seeing her not as a child, a tiresome young sister to be dragged into shape to meet the world, but as a woman, a potentially desirable woman, it was only fair to recognise that this altered situation could only put him under a strain that neither of them needed.

It was one thing for her to live under his roof as an old friend, on a platonic basis. They could both co-exist happily enough under that circumstance, as was intended. But for her to play on today's events would be an infringement of friendship, much less hospitality, and Helen knew she must never, never do that.

Dane obviously knew it, too. Because beginning the next morning he took pains to ensure there was no repeat performance. So tactfully, so subtly, that Helen wouldn't even have caught it if she hadn't known him so well, he managed to ensure a safety margin between them, a physical but invisible barrier that maintained their friendship without risk.

And the donkeys helped; in fact so did the entire menagerie. When Dane mentioned that he was going through a particularly bad patch with his latest novel, Helen gradually assumed the farm chores, which she quite enjoyed anyway, and found that she spent most of her days out-of-doors, while he stayed locked in his office. Their paths crossed only at meal times and on the occasional evening when they might sit companionably listening to music, reading, or watching the occasional television programme.

By the end of a fortnight, Helen had taken over the farm work almost in total, along with those aspects of the house not already handled—quite adequately—by the twice-weekly visits of a neighbour lady who did the laundry and washing and general house-cleaning.

It was difficult at first for Helen to be sure exactly what Mrs Bowen thought of her being there, but gradually it became clear that Dane was the woman's idol and could simply do no wrong. Helen's presence was, therefore, perfectly correct because it was at his instigation.

Helen also found that despite Dane's earlier objections, it was just as easy to gradually assume control of the kitchen. She did most of the cooking, all of the shopping for both home and farm, and quickly came to feel that she was anything but redundant.

The hardest part of it all was learning to find her way through Hobart's maze of one-way streets, on those few occasions when she had to go all the way into the city. For most things, she could shop quite conveniently in the community of Kingston, and she usually did just that.

Dane, having apologised once for his single-minded approach to this particular novel, seemed to take Helen's input for granted, but this didn't bother her as it might have earlier in her life. She knew her contribution was appreciated, and because she was so enjoying herself she hardly noticed the passage of time.

Almost every day, she rode Maria, then spent half an hour or so with each of the other donkeys, teaching them basic things like being groomed and handled and having their feet picked up and their hooves trimmed. Trumpet, as she'd expected, proved the most difficult of the quartet, being flighty and of rather uncertain temperament. Joshua was as docile as first impressions had indicated, and showed signs of becoming a most useful beast.

There were times when the ease with which she'd slipped into the routine bothered her. It was sometimes just too ... domestic, almost as if they were a married couple of long standing. Dane never questioned her expenditures, always tucked into her cooking with complimentary vigour, and always found time during the day to listen with interest and consideration to her reports about the animals' health and progress.

But he maintained that distance between them; whether because he was so wound up in his writing or because he just thought it necessary, Helen wasn't certain. And, most surprising of all, he never argued with her about anything. That was what she missed most, if anything. She had always enjoyed arguing with him, honing her vocabulary and her mind during discussions about anything and everything.

Then, without warning or preamble, he did begin arguing with her again, and it didn't take long until she was wishing he wouldn't.

'You remember that discussion we were having about somebody stepping into Vivian's shoes?' he asked one

evening after dinner when there was a fine fire going in
the lounge room and they were both settled with coffee
and liqueurs.

'I'm hardly likely to forget it, am I?' Helen replied,
not being bitchy or nasty, but obviously enough rather
surprised at the unexpected question. And, admittedly,
a trifle sarcastic.

But Dane ignored the sarcasm. 'And how do you feel
about it now that you've been here a while?' he asked.
'Still feel like there's a ghost in the house?'

'I never did,' Helen replied. 'That was, I thought, a
sort of hypothetical discussion in any case.'

'It still is,' he replied.

'Well I should hope so, which is the whole point. I'm
only here as a visitor. I can't look at this as if . . . well
. . . you know.'

'You could at least try and think of it that way,' he
insisted. 'I mean, it isn't all that far-fetched, surely.'

'Vivian would turn over in her grave,' Helen replied,
her voice slightly ragged from strain. Damn him!
Couldn't he see that this was one subject she simply
couldn't hypothesise about? She didn't dare! And then
she calmed herself. How could he see it . . . she hadn't
herself until he'd asked that question. But now that she
did . . .

'She would probably think it was marvellous,' he
said, not looking at her, not seeing the cruelty he was
inflicting.

Helen bit her lip, then spoke out brutally, knowing
she must nip this conversation in the bud before it
became any more involved, before she found herself
believing in it, believing in him despite his claim that it
was all hypothetical.

'She'd think it was incestuous. And so would I.'

'I see.' And now he was looking at her, through eyes
as cold and brittle as ice, eyes she couldn't continue to
meet. Helen dropped her gaze even as he continued.
'Yes, I suppose you would feel that way, wouldn't you?'

'Why not? You do.' And again her reply held an aura of frank brutality, but she couldn't help that. It was her only defence from allowing him to resume the discussion, to bring up possibilities she didn't dare to consider. Not after his bland assertion that it was all hypothetical.

'I was willing to set that aside ... for purposes of discussion,' Dane replied, voice calm despite the wildfire she could still see flickering in his eyes.

'Well I'm sorry, but I ... I can't,' she replied, 'especially not after ...' And she couldn't go on, couldn't put into words her feelings about that one, soul-destroying kiss. Dane was her friend, but he was more than that, and she simply couldn't! But he could.

'Not after a kiss that showed a modicum of mutual physical attraction? I can't see why that should matter, in theory.'

'I wasn't thinking about that,' Helen lied, making it up now as she went along and hoping she could slide the falsehoods past him so quickly he wouldn't notice. 'It's just that ... well ... I still feel very guilty about not being able to make Vivian's funeral, and about never really telling her how ... how grateful I was to her and ... and everything. And I just ... just can't talk so calmly about taking her place, not even hypothetically—which is a word I'm coming to hate, by the way—because nobody could ever take her place. She was, as I believe you said, unique.'

'Ah.' She didn't dare look at him, knowing he'd read the lie from her eyes. But when he didn't speak more than that single word, Helen finally was forced to look up, only he wasn't looking at her anyway. That surprised her.

And then he was, but there was none of the cold assessment she might have expected, and the wildfire was burned away now from his eyes. He was calm, perhaps too calm, considering her own rattled emotions.

'I don't know why it is that we invariably seem to get off on the wrong track every time I instigate a serious discussion,' he said. 'It must be me; we never used to do that. So let's just forget what's just been said, and see if we can manage to get round this in simple terms. I was hoping that you might spend a bit of time helping me design a new kitchen for this place, Helen. And what all the rest was leading up to is that I'd like you to approach the project as if it was a kitchen you were going to have to live with for a very long time.'

Now it was Helen's turn to say, 'Ah,' which was about all she could say, for the moment. She felt so stupid, so damned silly, that sensible words just wouldn't break through the glue that seemed to be holding her jaw shut.

'Very profound.' She could hear the sarcasm in his voice, but she didn't dare look to see it in his eyes.

'I . . . I suppose I could do that,' she finally managed to splutter. 'Although I really can't see the sense of it. I mean, it's perfectly liveable as it is, and wouldn't it be better to wait until, well, whoever's really going to have to live with it?'

'I've been doing that since I moved down here, and I'm sick of it,' he replied. 'It would have to be the most incompetently arranged kitchen on the face of the earth, as I'm sure you're well aware by now. Vivian hated it, and you'll come to hate it, too, in time.'

'Very likely,' Helen replied, eyes downcast to hide the thrill of pleasure that had surged up inside her at the merest suggestion that she'd be staying long enough for that to happen.

Actually, she had barely noticed the kitchen except during moments when the inconvenience was most noticeable. With only the two of them to feed, it served well enough for her culinary needs. Her major criticism would have been the southwestern exposure that kept the room from getting any sun at all during winter. And which, she thought, would make it unbearably hot at dinner time in summer.

And yet ... could she really ... *honestly* ... approach the project as he intended? As if she were going to have to live with the result for a long, long time? When she wasn't ... and worse ... knew she wasn't? Even though she was beginning to feel that she most desperately wanted to? Helen found her head spinning. It was unfair. Perhaps innocently so, but nonetheless unfair. And she couldn't even tell him that, not without revealing things she didn't dare to reveal. Not without altering their association, perhaps destructively, forever.

But there was no logical excuse, bar sheer ignorance, that she could offer for refusing to help in the design. And she knew Dane would see through any but the most thoroughly prepared of excuses, which she didn't have time to prepare anyway.

'Oh, all right. I'll at least think about it,' she finally, grudgingly conceded. 'But I really think you're mad to ask *me*. I'm certainly no architect; I'm not even all that much of a cook.'

'And you're overly modest,' Dane replied with a grin. 'Your cooking has improved out of sight from what I remember. As for not being an architect—I don't remember asking you to do this all by yourself. What I want is for you to help me get the thing worked out to the point where we can hand it over to an architect and know he's started on the right track, that's all.'

Which effectively ended any show of argument from Helen. A few minutes later, Dane retreated to the seclusion of his office with his usual reminder that he wasn't to be disturbed except in the most dire of emergencies, leaving Helen to ponder the rough sketches he'd left her of how the addition—including kitchen space—would look.

She sat at the kitchen table, staring at the sketches without really seeing them, wondering why he inevitably demanded there be no interruptions when there never were any in the first place. In all the time she'd been there, Helen recalled, the 'phone had rung only once while Dane was working, and that had been a wrong number.

She was still pondering that when the telephone's shrill bell jerked her back to reality, and she reached up to grasp at the receiver before the noise could further disturb Dane.

This time, it wasn't a wrong number, but it took Helen several moments of annoying conversation to determine that. Conversation, she decided later, that she'd rather have done without.

CHAPTER FOUR

'WHO's that?' It was an educated voice, but querulous with naked, obvious suspicion. Almost angry. And rude!

Unbidden, Helen's mind recalled an incident long in the past, when Dane had received a similar type of response to answering a 'phone, and without second thoughts she parroted his response of that time.

'Who wants to know?' Her reply was mildly flippant, but only sufficiently so to inform the unknown caller that Helen had no intention of being harassed. And it worked, marginally.

'I would like,' the voice purred, although the purr held the beginnings of a growl behind it, 'to speak to Dane Curtis.'

Not the slightest indication that the woman thought she might have a wrong number, nothing like that at all. She knew the number she'd dialled; it was hearing a woman's voice—Helen's voice—that had spawned the rude opening.

'I'm sorry,' Helen replied gently. 'He's not available just at the moment. May I take a message?'

'You may get him to the telephone . . . now!' And the purr had grown into a genuine snarl. Whomever this woman might be, she was quite obviously used to having her own way in all things. Even, Helen wondered, where Dane was concerned?

'I'm very sorry but I can't do that,' she replied, keeping her voice gentle, refusing to reveal the slightest provocation despite her urge to reply to rudeness with a bit of rudeness herself.

'Just who the hell do you think you are?' was the angry reply. And then the voice softened perceptibly.

'Now look, if he's there, I should like to speak to him. He will want to speak to me, I can assure you.'

Helen refused to be drawn.

'I'm sorry, but I can't do that,' she replied, then silently cursed as she realised that she should have instead continued to deny his availability. This opening, however slight, was enough for the angry caller to gain a foothold.

'Hah! So he *is* there,' the voice snapped, fierce now in the first chances of winning. 'And I suppose he's hiding in that den he calls an office, pleading overwork and demanding not to be disturbed except in the most dire of emergencies.'

It was too much in Dane's own words; this woman had obviously heard them before and Helen couldn't help wondering under just what circumstances. Not to mention wondering who the mysterious caller was ... For just an instant, Helen was stuck for a reply.

'But don't tell me he's hired a secretary to screen him from the wicked world outside,' the voice went on. 'I know you're not Mrs Bowen; she would have put me through without all this ... this ridiculous hedging.'

'No,' Helen replied. 'I'm not his secretary.' But she was damned if she'd bother to explain just who she was ... notwithstanding the fact that she wasn't entirely sure of that herself. She had a fair idea of the response if she were to describe herself to this caller as the property's resident jillaroo. She was tempted for an instant to say she was his mother, but such flippancy would hardly be appreciated once the woman did contact Dane, and Helen had no doubts that would be accomplished ... and fairly soon at that.

'But you're not going to let me talk to him?' It was hardly a question, and Helen was halfway through saying that she could only obey her instructions when the caller hung up on her.

'You are a very rude woman,' she muttered into the

silent receiver, half-wishing she'd said it when the woman was there to hear.

She remained in the kitchen for fifteen minutes, half convinced the telephone caller would try again, and yet not at all certain she wanted to be there when it happened. Then Helen decided she'd be more productive if she simply put the matter from her mind. When Dane finished working, or in the morning if she'd gone to bed before he did, she would mention the call to him. And somehow she knew that he'd need little prompting if any to figure out who'd called.

Then she yawned, glancing up at the kitchen clock and wondering how she could possibly be tired at only eight p.m. Ever since her arrival she'd found herself sleeping long hours, and wondered if it was some sort of biological adjustment to the cooler weather. Dane, Helen knew, had no such problem; he got by on five or six hours of sleep each night, while she seemed to need more like ten.

But to go to bed now . . . it was ridiculous and yet so tempting. Even if it did mean getting up before dawn, she thought, yawning again. Well, she could at least have her shower, and if it woke her up again it wouldn't be much of a crisis.

She was just emerging from the shower, hair pulled back by a rubber band and her face flushed from the heat, when Helen saw car lights swinging into the drive, and heard Molly's gruff warning bark as the vehicle approached.

'Oh . . . great,' she thought, shrugging into a house-coat and scrambling to find her slippers. It wasn't until the second knock on the door that she realised Dane wasn't going to answer; he was obviously waiting for her to do it.

Helen let the caller knock once more, then stalked through to fling open the door herself, mentally cursing Dane as she did so.

'Well.' Helen merely thought the word; the tall, dark-haired beauty outside the door seemed to breathe it out as if she was savouring the very texture of the word and anything it might imply.

There were several instantly descriptive words for this woman, Helen thought, the first of them being elegant. But she would have to add in haughty, almost regal, in fact, and certainly beautiful.

A flowing mane of dark hair, eyes like those of some great cat, quite aristocratic features. Thirty, perhaps a few years over. And certainly the woman who'd 'phoned earlier; the single word was sufficient to tell Helen that.

But what to do now? Hardly a matter of great choice, Helen thought. She might be able to fob off a telephone caller, but having arrived in person, there was little doubt the woman fully intended to reach Dane. Still, she had to give it a try.

'May I help you?' she asked politely. 'Are you lost, or . . .'

'Oh, don't be difficult, for goodness' sake,' the tall sultry woman muttered, shooting Helen a scathing glance as she almost pushed her aside in striding through the door.

And once inside, headed straight for Dane's office. Clearly, Helen thought, the woman had been here before. And equally clearly, she herself was about to bow out of this entire scenario. Try as she might, Helen couldn't imagine herself attempting to physically restrain the visitor.

It was a decision thankfully forestalled by Dane stepping through the doorway even as his visitor reached out for the handle. And he didn't—Helen realised immediately—appear nearly as surprised as could be reasonably expected under the circumstances.

'Well, this is a surprise. What are you doing running around in the middle of the night, Marina?' It looked and sounded perfect, but Helen wasn't fooled and she doubted seriously if this Marina was, either.

'I tried to 'phone, but this ... person refused to let me speak to you,' was the reply. 'You've been keeping secrets from me, darling. Here I thought you were slaving over a hot typewriter; that is what you said you'd be doing. And instead I find you've been ... entertaining?'

Helen flinched at the naked innuendo, and even more so at the smooth, purring cattiness of the tone. Again she had the feeling that there was something inordinately feline about this woman, especially when one manicured finger stretched out to stroke a path along Dane's forearm.

Definitely cat, Helen thought, seeing in her mind that finger with a claw withdrawn only enough to be polite, but still revealed enough to proclaim a form of dangerous possessiveness.

'This ... person, is Helen Fredericks, an old friend and now a sort of house-guest,' Dane replied, seemingly ignorant of the spell this woman appeared to be trying to weave. 'Helen, this is Marina Cole, and if you did put her off on the 'phone, don't feel badly about it, because you were only doing what I'd asked.'

But not, Helen couldn't help thinking, what he'd really wanted. No, if he'd known the identity of the caller, he'd have been on the 'phone like a flash. Or ... would he? Suddenly she realised that far from being ignorant of Marina's tactics, he was actually playing to her tune deliberately. But why?

'And of course, hearing a female voice, you just had to rush out and find for yourself what was going on,' he was saying to the brunette. 'Curiosity, dear Marina ... remember what it did to the cat.'

'Then it couldn't have been much of a cat,' Marina replied casually. Too casually, Helen thought, envying the woman her style.

And also her clothing sense, Helen thought, suddenly realising the contrast between her own rather ancient housecoat and Marina's expensive casual-elegant pant suit. It was time, she thought then, to take herself out of this.

'If you'll excuse me,' she said quietly. 'I was just getting ready for bed.'

Marina's expression clearly—at least to another woman—asked whose bed, but Dane interjected before anything else could be said. 'Oh, come and have a drink with us first,' he said. 'It's too early for bed, surely.'

And if it hadn't been for that questioning look on the other woman's face, Helen might have refused. But now she wouldn't. Instead, she determined to make herself the gooseberry just out of spite, because she definitely did not like Marina Cole and knew beyond doubt the feelings were reciprocated.

'All right. I'll be with you in a minute,' she said then, and dashed to her room to emerge with her hair combed and wearing a set of pale yellow lounging pajamas cut just low enough in front to give her a vague advantage over the tailored style of Marina's outfit.

Dane hadn't seen this outfit; she was usually attired in very casual jeans and sweatshirt around the house. But he liked it immediately, she could tell that despite his failure to make any verbal comment.

Her drink was waiting, and she curled up in a corner of the sofa with it, just close enough to be included in the conversation to follow, but far enough away that she could remain more of an observer than a direct participant if the opportunity offered.

Marina, with one cat-eyed glance, told Helen she'd have preferred the tattered housecoat, and even more have preferred Helen's absence from the room, the house, the property and even Tasmania. No question; it was that kind of look.

'The reason I stopped by was not, as you so rudely put it, simply curiosity,' Marina was saying, one hand busily touching Dane, deliberately establishing a physical intimacy for nobody's benefit but Helen's. 'But to remind you of the party on Saturday. You did promise you'd come, remember. Mother would be so very disappointed if you've changed your mind.'

'Did I promise? Goodness, Marina, that was months ago ... I can't really remember,' Dane was saying. 'Certainly before I knew that Helen was coming, anyway.'

'Oh, but that doesn't matter. Of course she must come to the party as well. Plenty of room.' Marina seemed just slightly condescending for an instant, then confirmed Helen's suspicion. 'And there'll be a *few* people there her own age, I'm sure, including one or two quite eligible young men.'

Helen seethed, trying not to show it, But Dane merely laughed, the sound ringing in the now-tense atmosphere.

'Lining dear Helen up with appropriate young men is the last thing I hope to get involved with,' he chuckled. 'She's more than capable of finding her own, thank you very much.'

'Not if you insist on keeping her locked away out here in the scrub,' Marina replied calmly, but there was a steely glint in those bland cat's eyes. 'Unless, of course, that's the whole idea. Is she ... hiding from something? Or someone?'

The brunette waited only long enough to have made her point; she didn't expect an answer and that, too, was clear. 'Seriously, Dane, what *is* she doing here?' Marina asked then, as if the earlier questions had been only jokes. And, Helen thought, as if she, herself, was incapable of handling direct inquisition.

'I'm just sort of the resident jillaroo,' she blurted before Dane could reply. 'You know ... milk the goats, slop the hogs, that sort of thing.'

Marina never batted an eye. 'How ... quaint,' she murmured, not even bothering to glance over as Helen spoke. It was, just in two words, the total put-down, the ultimate in condescension.

But if Dane noticed, and Helen was sure he must, he ignored that aspect of the comment. 'Helen understates the situation,' he said. 'Actually, she does just about everything around here but write my books for me.'

And there was something, something barely audible in his inflexion of *everything*. Something that caused Helen's heart to tumble like a wounded bird, and Marina Cole's eyes to narrow in speculation, then widen in ill-disguised fury.

'She sounds utterly perfect,' the brunette finally said, the words emerging almost in a hiss. 'I'm hardly surprised, now, that you told me you'd be isolating yourself so you could finish your latest book. Although,' and she paused dramatically but only for an instant, 'I'm also rather surprised that you haven't married her if she's so perfect.'

And Dane ... Dane laughed. A great, boisterous, rollicking burst of laughter that caught both women by surprise. Then he spoke, and the words landed like lumps of lead on Helen's fluttering heart.

'It's got to be out of the question,' Dane said. 'She's practically family. It would be incestuous.'

And did he glance at her when he said that final word? Helen thought he might have, but with her own eyes averted as her mind skipped through what he was saying, must say, she couldn't be certain. Certainly, however, she didn't need help to interpret the flickering expression of pure relief that flashed across Marina's beautiful features.

But Helen, herself, had to speak out. Had to use words to scour the pain from inside her, use words as a defence against the hurt. No matter how much more hurt it caused her.

'If that's the best kind of story you can dream up, then maybe I *should* be writing your books for you,' she scoffed, throwing Dane a dazzling smile. 'Why don't you tell Miss Cole the truth, that I'm an unemployed journalist whom you've taken pity on for old times' sake, and that you soothe my conscience by keeping me busy with all sorts of little farm jobs?'

Helen would have continued, but her throat stuck. Words piled up behind her tongue ... harsh, unkind, untrue words. Defensive words that would only worsen her position. Because really, what was there to say? It was the truth; she was staying here as an object of pity, no more than an old friend being helped over a rough patch in life.

'And speaking of farm jobs, I think now you must excuse me,' she finally managed to say. 'The donkeys get up early, and I'll have to, as well.'

She was out of the room, fleeing, ashamed of it but unable to handle any other course of action, almost before Dane and his lady friend could reply. It wasn't until she was safely in her room that Helen could afford to release the pent-up fury of her emotions, cursing silently into a pillow that soaked up words and tears with equal ease.

When Dane, some time later, saw Marina off and then paused to knock softly on Helen's door, she pretended not to hear. And when morning arrived, she was out working the donkeys almost before the arrival of the sun, shivering in the cold air but knowing she'd feel even colder inside the house.

Helen knew very well it hadn't been Dane's comments which had so upset her, nor even the dark-haired woman's condescending attitude. The problem was her own attitude. She was too vulnerable, too easily hurt, too tender.

But worse was the realisation that her time here was now limited. She couldn't—mustn't—stay any longer than was absolutely necessary. Only ... where could she go? With no job and no money, there wasn't a lot of choice except home to mother, and that was simply too horrendous to consider.

'So I'll have to find a job; that's all there is to it,' she muttered, leaning momentarily against the fence and watching the sun glitter against the sea far to the east. 'I don't have to be a journalist, although it would be best.'

And immediately resolved to collect the various weekend papers that Saturday ... all of them. Surely somewhere in Australia there would be a job for her, a means of escape before her involvement with Dane Curtis made escape impossible.

It was nearly noon, and the day already unseasonably warm, when Helen returned to the house, drawn, in part, by the unmistakable sound of someone splitting firewood. As she rounded the corner of the yard, the sound became louder and she paused, unable to resist the pleasure of watching Dane engrossed in his labour.

He was stripped to the waist, the sun glistening on a muscular chest and back as he rhythmically swung the splitting axe to slice great rounds of log into neat sections of stove wood.

Watching him, seeing the economy of effort, the pure mixture of strength and skill, the involved play of muscles and sinew, Helen felt a great emptiness inside her.

He was, and no denying it, a man of supreme sexual attractiveness with his lithe, thoroughly co-ordinated movements. Not the over-muscled build of a weight-lifter, but the body of a competitive swimmer, where strength and suppleness combined to create beauty.

And he was, she now realised, a great deal leaner than she remembered, now had all the sedentary softness driven from his body. He was hard and fit and trim ... and too desirable by half.

And also, she discovered very quickly, too observant.

'Are you buying something, or just window-shopping?' he asked, pausing only long enough to throw her a quick, mildly sarcastic grin. 'If you've nothing better to do than stand around admiring the body beautiful, you might as well get busy stacking some of this wood so I've got room to move here.'

'Actually, I was merely wondering how those sedentary writer's muscles could stand the strain of such heavy work,' Helen retorted, lying boldly to cover the confusion she felt at having been caught.

'And I suppose you think you could do better? Okay, here,' he replied, striding over to hand her the heavy, wedge-shaped implement. 'You reckon you're so tough, get to it. I'll just have a smoke, somewhere over here a safe distance away.'

She had to laugh, although silently and secretively. Dane had, for once, caught himself out. She knew from long childhood experience how to handle this aspect of country life, and although she hadn't his strength, she knew the tricks of splitting wood. Knew them all, and quickly found she hadn't forgotten.

Long before his cigarette was finished, she had honed the old skills and was rending the chunks of log nearly as neatly as he had done. Helen continued at the task, revelling in the work, until Dane finally called to her to stop.

'That'll do, thank you,' he finally said. 'Splitting firewood is *my* therapy, and if you expect me to sit and watch you do it, then the least you could do is be properly dressed.'

'What's the matter with the way I'm dressed?' She had the question asked before his wolfish grin revealed his meaning. And then, just for an instant, she was tempted . . . oh, so tempted.

'I wouldn't,' he cautioned. 'You'd give Mrs Bowen a shock from which she might never recover. And I'm not sure I could handle it either, so why don't you go see about some lunch instead.'

'Chauvinist!' Helen cried. 'You couldn't care less if I worked topless or not; you just can't handle the fact that I can do the work as well as you.'

'Which you wouldn't be, if you were out here topless,' he retorted. 'Or at least, not for long. Now run along, dear Helen, before I show you one of the other uses a piece of firewood can be put to and you have to eat lunch standing up.'

And he advanced slowly, one hand extended to take the splitting axe from her. But instead of handing it to him, Helen laid the implement down between them, then as quickly grabbed it up again and scampered clockwise around the woodpile.

Dane grinned, and it was a wolfish, cunning grin. Then he stooped to pick up a slender wand of scrap wood and advanced upon her again, his intent now beyond question.

'You come near me with that and I'll drop this axe on your foot,' Helen warned. 'I mean it.'

And she would have, except that to manoeuvre the fifteen-pound splitting axe *that* quickly was simply beyond her strength and agility. Dane easily evaded her first and only try, then plucked the axe from her fingers and pulled her close against him almost in the same motion.

He'd dropped the sliver of firewood, too, so that both hands were free to close round her waist, pulling her tight against him in a vice-like grip that she couldn't oppose.

'You are a naughty child, young Helen,' he murmured in her ear, but Helen was more aware of the crush of his warm chest against her, of the strong, hot pressure of his loins.

'And you really do deserve a spanking,' he continued, one hand releasing its grip only long enough to land with a resounding smack on her rump, drawing forth a squeal of surprise, more than outright indignation.

'I have never seen such unmitigated jealousy as you showed last night,' he continued, following up the comment with yet another smack.

'Childish, ridiculous, quite unprecedented jealousy.' Smack!

'Particularly from someone who maintains that we don't have that kind of relationship.' Smack!

Helen would have spoken, would have shouted at him now in her indignant rage, but he was holding her too tightly. After every smack at her bottom, he would crush her against him again with both arms, effectively forcing the very air from her lungs, making any attempt at speech impossible.

And he was angry. Angrier than she was; Helen had no doubts about that. Angry with a cold, deliberate anger that she now realised he'd been taking out on the woodpile. Until she'd arrived. Anger that might have been exhausted against inert wood, but anger that without question had been directed squarely at her. And anger that had only been fanned white-hot by her intrusion.

'So maybe it's time you learned that teasing isn't the good sport you thought,' he continued, not bothering for some reason to follow that sentence with a smack. But he was far from finished.

'Bottomless can be worse than topless,' he growled. And added another smack to emphasise his point. 'But there are even worse things than either one.'

And now his lips took over the torture, capturing her mouth without warning, claiming her like some savage warrior, drinking in her breathlessness, savouring her helplessness.

Against the onslaught, her mouth trembled, then surrendered with hardly a fight. Her arms stole round his neck, holding herself tight to him; her breasts were crushed against his chest, but her nipples throbbed, growing with the heat of him, expanding, seeking.

The warmth of his naked torso was like a torch, alighting her passions, drawing from within her a fire that scorched at her body. Her fingers, now straying across the muscular width of his shoulders, radiated that heat. As did his own fingers, moving like quicksilver along the nubbles of her spine, touching first at the narrowness of her waist, then at the swelling curves of her hips.

Then his fingers were up beneath the softness of her jumper, their warmth vivid against her naked flesh. And she was holding him with her lips, meeting his kisses

with mounting urgency as his right hand slid along her
ribs, then up to cup her breast in a touch so exquisitely
gentle and yet so arousing that she gasped.

Somehow, the jumper lifted, and their bodies were
touching, burning, merging in a spreading warmth that
flowed through her in breathless haste. Her knees
weakened; only the strength of her arms now held her
upright against him.

She could feel the masculine strength of him against
her thighs, the warmth, the urgency. And her body
couldn't help but respond to the pull of his arm around
her waist, the light touch of his free hand at the
waistband of her jeans.

'Oh . . . God!' she sighed, feeling the light tracery of
fingers towards the very centre of her being, feeling her
body shift ever so slightly to accommodate his
searching hand.

She wanted him. Desperately. Immediately. Now!
Here! She wanted nothing more than for him to lower
her to the pungent bed of sawdust and woodchips, to
take her with a rising passion that matched her own.
Beneath her fingers, the curling hair at the nape of his
neck, then the mat across his chest, his stomach. Her
own fingers encountered a belt, soft denim, the core of
the flame that surged between them.

She heard his voice, soft in her ear, murmuring,
whispering words she couldn't hear, couldn't understand, and yet fully understood. And then another
voice, this one distant, strident, intruding. And his voice
again, this time fully audible.

'Damn!'

And her feet hit the ground with a thud as he
virtually dropped her, turning away as he did so to meet
the urgency of that other voice, Mrs Bowen's voice
calling him to the 'phone.

But it was Dane's voice that stayed with her as he
stalked away, his every movement taut with anger, but
also with . . . rejection?

'Just as bloody well, dear Helen. That was one lesson that very nearly came unstuck.'

A lesson! Her heart dropped like a stone from the previous dizzying heights to a rocky landing in reality. He might have wanted her. Had wanted her! But only as a lesson, only in a manner tinged with revenge for her teasing.

Helen snatched up the wood-splitting axe, fighting against the tears and anger and fury that merged with her despair. Twirling it before her, she brought the axe down with a sickening thud in the nearest chunk of wood, feeling that her heart must have landed with just such a sound, that her dreams were rent as was the round of log now evenly divided at her feet.

'Bastard!' She repeated the word over and over, punctuating it with perfectly timed, viciously effective blows of the axe. An hour later, she was still saying it, the words gasping out now, and the pile of split firewood beside her almost head high. But she didn't feel one damn bit better. And Dane, perhaps wisely, hadn't returned.

Nor was he in evidence when she finally abandoned *his* therapy as useless and returned to the house, ignoring the mildly curious glance from Mrs Bowen as she slammed through to her room and eventually to the shower.

Mrs Bowen, thankfully, had left for the day when Helen answered the door to a floral delivery youth and wonderingly accepted the dozen roses he extended with a warm smile. Helen's language when she read the note that accompanied the flowers would surely have given the elderly housekeeper a seizure.

'It was a dumb trick and I'm sorry, I think,' said the note. Helen's reply, shouted into emptiness through a veil of tears she could no longer contain, was far less gentle.

But when Dane finally did return, hours later, she managed to restrain herself, greeting him as if nothing had happened, laying the table for dinner silently, but not sullenly and able—just barely—to meet his eyes as they ate. Neither of them mentioned the earlier incident, but it was there, looming like a wraith in the tension-laden air.

And it was there, inside Helen's still-sensitive body, each time he moved, each time that movement revealed a flow of muscle, a disturbing memory of touch, of voice. When he shifted into his office almost immediately after the meal, Helen was both relieved and vaguely disappointed.

Next morning, it was easier ... slightly. Dane had risen before her, and when Helen woke after a surprisingly restful night, she found that most of the chores were already done and most of the previous night's tensions had been stilled.

'I'll just finish up and then we'll eat and be off,' Dane said with a smile when she met him outside the barn. 'I think we've both been cooped up out here too long, so we'll trot into town and visit the Salamanca markets, if that's okay with you?'

'Why not?' she replied noncommittally, deliberately hiding the excitement inside her. She had wanted to visit the open-air markets ever since hearing about them, but until now Dane had never so much as mentioned an interest.

He made up for this lapse as they drove through early-morning mists along the Southern Outlet and into the city. Although the weekly open-air market was in itself a primary tourist attraction, he said, the historic Salamanca warehouses, built of native stone between 1835 and 1860, had their own claim to fame.

Protected by cliffs created when a new wharf was constructed and later named Prince's Wharf to commemorate the visit in 1868 by Prince Alfred, the warehouses were once the commercial centre of Hobart Town, and still provided a stepping stone to the exploration of historic Battery Point, one of Tasmania's most unique tourist areas.

When they arrived, and during the expected struggle to find a parking space near the markets, Helen was struck by the beauty of the elderly buildings, but more so by the frenzied activity of the market itself. Sprawling through blocks of cobbled pavement which Dane told her was normally just parking for the warehouse area, the market teemed with life and activity.

She could see, as they strolled towards it, a kaleidoscope of booths and caravans selling everything from books to vegetables. Second-hand furniture, clothing, food and drink, arts and crafts were displayed seemingly without rhyme or reason, with the booths rising like islands from the sea of thronging early-morning shoppers that teemed around them.

'There is no possible way of staying together in this mess,' Dane muttered in her ear. 'I'll meet you in an hour outside the Ball and Chain,' pointing to a restaurant across the way. 'And then, if you're game to face the masses once again, we'll make new arrangements. Okay?'

Helen nodded, then plunged into the throng, letting herself be carried by the tide of shoppers and tourists as it swarmed along the pavement.

The next hour passed in a moment. She found that much of what was on offer could only be called junk, but there were other stalls that definitely interested her. Only once during that time did she even catch a glimpse of Dane, head bent over the wares of a second-hand book stall.

Helen also found the book stalls interesting, but it was so crowded in the market that she found it impossible to really investigate the books on offer. Not, at any rate, without more pushing and shoving for position that she could be bothered with.

Still, when she met Dane at the appointed time and place, she was flushed with excitement, an excitement generated in part by the sheer aliveness of the place, the bustle and the crowding and the voices.

Dane's face registered a tolerant amusement, perhaps tinged with boredom, but he merely smiled when she pointed first at herself, then at the throng behind her, and lifted one finger in the air. One more hour. Agreed. Helen slid back into the flow, this time with a definite purpose in mind.

Even so, it took her fifteen minutes to work her way back to the one second-hand clothing stall she'd especially noticed, and even longer to fully investigate the astonishing find she'd noticed in passing.

It was old, very old. A Victorian gown, she thought, but in amazingly good condition. The high-necked, many-buttoned bodice nipped to a tiny waist before flowing out again into the full skirt fashionable at the time. No bustle, she thought idly, and chuckled to herself as she held the garment before her, mentally calculating the fit. The dark, forest green colour that had first attracted her was flattering, and she could see where a few miniscule repairs would bring the garment back to life with relative ease. If it would fit!

'It's very fetching, love,' grinned the hawker, himself resplendent in a costume mingling eras from Victorian to modern and looking more like some strange court jester than a weekend merchant. 'I reckon you'll have to have it.'

'Not at this price, I won't,' she retorted gaily, instinctively realising that this man's prices were negotiable, provided one had the nerve to haggle. 'Besides, how can you expect me to buy something when there's nowhere to try it on?'

His ribald reply drew raised eyebrows from two older ladies passing, but Helen could only laugh at the man's impudence; it was so totally in keeping with his costume.

They haggled back and forth, cheerfully and without malice, for ten minutes before Helen finally agreed to pull the garment on over her street clothing. It wouldn't give her a perfect judgment of fit, especially not with her own shirt under it, but finally she decided that if he'd drop the price a bit more she would take the chance.

When she finally rejoined Dane for the second time, she had a paper-wrapped parcel tucked under one arm and was convinced that given the afternoon to work on it, she might even have the dress ready for the party being given that night by Marina's mother.

If I decide to go, she thought, having already tossed that particular issue over several times without resolution. All of her common sense cried out for her to plead a headache or any other excuse to avoid the party. She would only be out of place and, she knew only too well, made to feel it. But there was a mischievous imp inside that demanded equal time, demanded that she attend the party and do it with a style that might somehow mollify the humiliation she'd endured since meeting the elegant brunette.

This dress, if only it fit as well as she hoped, would go a long way in the right direction. It had ... style; style and a sense of history. A sense of rightness, somehow.

CHAPTER FIVE

FROM Helen's viewpoint, the party was immensely successful even before she arrived, The effect of the dress accounted for that.

She'd spent all afternoon in a frenzy of repairing, washing and pressing the garment, then rearranging hair and make-up to match the effect created. And it had all worked!

It was, she decided after staring almost with disbelief into the mirror, as if the dress had been created especially for her. It fitted perfectly, hugging her figure where that effect was intended, flowing like a cape of rich, dark moss below the hips. With her hair piled high and a minimum of make-up, her only jewellery an old brooch of her mother's, she left her room to find Dane standing in the lounge, a drink in his hand and another, presumably for her, on the table beside him.

He glanced up at her approach, raised one eyebrow in appreciation, then gave her a courtly bow as he handed over the drink.

'Now that,' he said, without a trace of anything but honest compliment, 'is absolutely astonishing. Fantastic!'

'It isn't bad, is it?' Helen replied, twirling in a perky little pirouette but being careful not to spill the drink in her hand. 'I'm actually rather proud of myself; it came out much better than I'd expected.'

'Well so you should be,' he replied. 'I've never seen you looking so . . . elegant.'

'And the same to you,' Helen replied. Honestly, because it was true. Dane was indeed elegant in his dinner jacket, his white dress shirt gleaming against the dark tan of his skin.

As they drove northwards towards Hobart, Helen leaned back into the softness of the car seat, glowing with an inner warmth at Dane's obvious approval of the job she'd done on the dress. But it was Marina Cole's reaction—when they arrived at the swank home in the trendy suburb of Sandy Bay—that capped Helen's evening.

'What a . . . marvellously original outfit,' Marina said upon greeting them upon her arrival. And the look in her eye said even more than the brittle tones of her voice. She didn't like Helen, and didn't like the dress even more, Helen knew. Just as she knew that nothing this woman might say or do tonight would be allowed to spoil her evening.

'You look very elegant yourself,' Helen responded, using honesty as her best defence and hoping she wouldn't need any other. With her dark colouring, Marina's choice of a flame-red gown gave the other woman a sultry, almost torrid look. Like a close-banked fire, Helen thought, not at all warmed by the analogy.

When she met Marina's mother, she could see where heredity had played a strong part in providing the raven-haired woman's classic beauty. Only years differentiated between Marina and her mother when it came to the fine bone structure, the elegant carriage. But on first impressions, she thought it unlikely Marina had inherited her mother's natural charm and graciousness. Her smile was warm and friendly, her attitude entirely one of welcome. Especially, Helen thought, for Dane.

'You've become too much a stranger,' Mrs Cole criticised in friendly tones as she led Dane and Helen round, introducing them to the various other guests. After a few moments, Helen found it no longer possible to keep track of the names or even the faces, but Dane seemed to know at least some of the other guests already.

As they drifted casually from group to group, Mrs
Cole having disappeared temporarily to greet new
arrivals, Dane was welcomed warmly, especially by the
ladies in the crowd. Several of the men, Helen was
pleased to notice, seemed more inclined to pay attention
to her. And just as well, she thought at one point, when
all the guests had apparently arrived and Marina felt
herself free to monopolise Dane entirely.

She was rather surprised, some time later, when
Marina—alone and seemingly quite deliberately so—
approached and drew her to a quiet corner. The other
woman's attitude was too gracious, too friendly; Helen
found herself immediately suspicious, and with good
reason, she thought, once the supposedly subtle
interrogation began.

'I didn't realise you'd known Dane for such a long
time,' Marina began. 'And did you know his wife very
well too?'

'Fairly well,' Helen replied, not really sure what reply
was expected of her. Whatever, there was more to this
line of questioning than met the eye, she thought, and
determined to watch her replies carefully. What did
Marina want? An *entrée* into Dane's taste in women?
Surely not, Helen thought.

'He must have cared for her a great deal,' Marina
continued, and all of Helen's journalistic training was
stirred by the ever-so careful shielding, the cautious
choosing of words, inflection, nuance.

'I think it would be fair to say she was the centre of
his universe,' Helen replied, choosing words carefully
herself and totally alert to the reactions they might
cause. 'But . . . surely he'd have told you that himself?'

Marina, the defender now, managed without a flicker
of muscle to appear nonchalant about her reply. 'Of
course,' she said, 'although to be honest he seldom
mentions her. I thought it was . . . because she and I are
. . . somewhat alike?'

And she hadn't meant for the statement to emerge as

a question, Helen realised. Indeed, Marina probably didn't realise it had. But Helen did! In her ears the question mark at the end was louder than the words ahead of it.

She's fishing, Helen thought, and wondered only briefly why. Obviously it was because Dane hadn't, and from her own knowledge of him, wouldn't have discussed his dead wife with Marina Cole or anyone else who hadn't known Vivian personally.

To Dane, such action would be almost unthinkable, unless of course things between he and Marina had progressed to the point where such confidences had a place. And if that were the case, Helen immediately realised, the brunette wouldn't be asking her these questions at all.

But how to answer? Anything she said now might be wrong, either by breaking confidence with Dane or by deliberately antagonising one of his friends. No matter what she said, it could so easily be taken wrongly.

'I ... well, I really couldn't say,' she finally stammered. 'She was very special to me, you see. Almost an older sister, in some respects, and I'm ... I'm afraid I couldn't ... well, I couldn't think in terms of such comparisons.'

'Of course, I understand completely,' Marina replied, but the unholy glow in her eyes seemed to Helen anything but understanding or compassionate. She found herself suppressing a shiver, knowing that somehow she'd slipped up, somehow she'd made the wrong reply, and that somehow she'd pay the price for not thinking more quickly, more clearly. Probably, she thought, the price would be paid before this night was over. And the party began to lose its glow even before Marina's next question jangled warning bells Helen couldn't possibly disregard.

'Of course, it must be ... very difficult for you now,' Marina was saying. 'I mean, holding on to such memories now that you don't really think of Dane as being quite . . . brotherly?'

'I'm afraid I don't know what you mean,' Helen lied, fighting to keep voice and expression as blandly innocent and knowing she couldn't maintain it for long.

'Oh, I think you do,' Marina replied, a knowing sneer barely hidden. 'And one could hardly blame you, I suppose, although heaven knows it must be difficult enough competing with a ghost without adding incestuous memories into the exercise. And . . . especially when you must realise you can't possibly win.'

'What *are* you talking about?' Helen asked. Knowing, but forced to deny it both to her haughty interrogator and to herself. 'There's nothing between Dane and myself, if that's what you're getting at. And there never has been.'

'Of course,' Marina smiled, a panther's smile, a cat-like, animal smile so filled with innuendo, with disbelief, that it seemed her gleaming teeth dripped venom.

Worse, her attitude seemed somehow capable of besmirching Helen's true relationship with Dane, seemed to dirty it, to create in Helen a feeling of self-loathing that she didn't feel, and yet somehow did.

Again, Helen had to suppress a shudder of distaste, a feeling, a knowledge, even, that beside this woman she was too naïve, too innocent in the ways of womankind. The confidence brought to her by the dress, by Dane's reaction to it, drained away beneath the gaze of Marina's feline eyes.

'What are you two conspiring about, all hidden away in the corner like this?' Dane's voice, so unexpected, almost made Helen leap in fright, but Marina showed no such signs of guilt.

'Girl talk, darling,' she replied, a malicious smile— evident at least to Helen—playing across her vivid lips. But it was the remainder of her statement that struck at Helen like a whip-lash, ripping into the tenderness of her situation in a single cruel blow.

'Actually, we've been discussing your wicked past,' Marina said. 'And your young Helen has been telling me all about you and . . . Vivian!'

Helen gasped, unable to accept the deliberateness of the lie. Then she looked up at Dane, pleading with her eyes, her entire face, for him to look at her, to see the lie for what it was. But he wasn't looking at Helen, and only the slight twitching of the muscles at his jaw line revealed how he might have taken the remark.

'Well I'd watch it, if I were you, Marina,' he said, voice soft, silken, coldly angry to Helen's ear yet purring with the charm he could so easily assume. 'Because *my young Helen* has been known to lie, on occasion,' he continued, and the sound of her name from his lips was touched with bitterness, burned with acid as sharp as Helen's own fear.

And his eyes, which now met Helen's in a brief, undeniably fleeting glance, were as cold as the grave. Helen summoned up all of her courage, wanting to deny the malicious charge, needing to deny it, but unable to find the words before Dane took Marina by the arm and strolled back towards the centre of the party.

'Bitch!' Helen spat silently at the departing brunette. 'Bitch . . . bitch . . . bitch . . .' But there was no one to hear the silently-mouthed words, and nobody to soften the sickening, sinking feeling that plunged through Helen's midriff like an icy dagger.

For the rest of the evening, Helen felt that Dane was ignoring her, perhaps deliberately because of what he thought she might have confided to Marina, or perhaps just because his hostess's daughter was once again monopolising his time.

Helen didn't really know and wasn't really sure she cared. All she wanted to do was to leave, to go home, to free herself from the aura of malignancy that now seemed to surround her. That Marina could lie so deliberately and so easily didn't now surprise her, but it was devastating to think that Dane could be so easily taken in by the lie.

Obviously, she thought, he was much more tender, much more vulnerable in his loss of Vivian than she'd ever imagined, or he wouldn't be reacting this way, wouldn't be so easily stirred up by Vivian's memory and the possibility of Helen saying something about her.

And yet . . . what could he think Helen might say? She knew of nothing that *could* be said against Vivian, even if she might be so callous as to speak ill of the dead, which she definitely was not! And the little she had told Marina was no more than the truth. Vivian had been the centre of Dane's universe. He had loved her totally, completely. And had never denied it during her life-time, so why should he feel obliged now to fight shy of Helen speaking about what had been a good marriage, an excellent marriage?

Unless, she thought, he was growing close enough to Marina that he didn't want Vivian's ghost to step into the picture. That might very well explain his sudden coldness. Vivian might . . . must . . . exist in the relationship between herself and Dane, because Vivian was a part of both their memories. But if Marina had never met Vivian, and could therefore not be tied to her in Dane's mind by tentacles from the past—as Helen was—then perhaps he wanted to keep it that way, to be able to separate in his mind the two women.

She thought about it, mulling it around, twisting and turning it in her mind like some cat's-cradle of tenuous thought, even while she was carrying on conversations with other party guests, even while she fended off the obvious attentions of two different male guests who might have greatly interested her—at another time and in another place.

And it was still holding pride-of-place in her mind when the time came—finally!—for them to leave, for her to face being alone with Dane in the car, in his home, and to face at least one attempt to convince him that she *hadn't* been betraying any confidences, that Marina had led her into a trap and snapped it shut with a masterly, vicious gesture.

'We *weren't* talking about Vivian, you know,' Helen began, hardly waiting until the car was in motion before she let the words burst from her.

Dane said nothing. He drove with both hands neatly balanced on the steering wheel, both eyes intent on the road before him, alert to the demands of the light traffic around them. And he should have answered, could have at least acknowledged her remark, Helen thought.

'Didn't you hear me?' she was finally forced to ask, spitting out the words now, angry with both herself and with him. Hating Marina, but hating herself too for being so gullible, so easily trapped.

'I heard you.' A flat, calm, expressionless statement that told her less than nothing. He had heard her. So what?

'But you don't believe me.' And while she tried not to sound hurt, not to sound wounded by his lack of faith, she didn't try *too* hard. Not that it mattered.

'Why should I not believe you?' he replied, still in flat tones, still with nothing to guide her in assessing his meaning, his true feelings.

'Because obviously you think I'm a liar,' she replied, angry now and not hesitant about showing it. 'You said so; you told your sultry little friend that specifically.'

'Ah ... is that what's bugging you?' he replied. 'I thought it was something important.'

'You don't consider it important when you call somebody a liar?'

'I didn't call you a liar, you know,' he said. 'I said that you have been known to lie on occasions, which isn't the same thing at all.'

'Well I fail to see the difference.'

His only reply was a half-grunt that might have been

affirmative or the total opposite. And in the silence which followed, he made no comment to clarify that.

Helen sat there, eyes burning with tears she daren't let go, watching the lights of Hobart go past, seeing cars approach, then disappear past them, seeing nothing, really, because she wasn't looking.

How could he possibly be so obtuse? Except, of course, quite deliberately. As the silent drive continued, Helen became more and more certain that he was deliberately punishing her, and worse, that he was even enjoying it.

But why? Once again, she was overcome by the question of why it should matter to Dane whether she discussed Vivian with the treacherous Marina or anyone else, for that matter. It wasn't as if she could say anything against Vivian, and he must know that. Nor was there any logical reason for him to object because he fancied that his memories should remain sacred; she'd been asked for her own impressions. And yet . . . how had Marina so accurately known that she could put Helen in the wrong just by mentioning it? That, she decided, was the real question!

And for Helen it was a question without an answer. Dane obviously wasn't going to provide one. Obviously wasn't going to provide answers to anything, judging by his stern silence as they drove steadily southward, leaving the city lights behind them.

Damn him! 'Is that all you're going to say about it?' she suddenly demanded.

His shrug was maddening. 'What else do you want me to say?'

'Well, you might at least admit that you're deliberately being close-mouthed about this, that you're deliberately leading me on, although for the life of me I don't know why,' Helen replied.

'Oh, might I?' And he was, she realised, only barely holding back a blatant chuckle. He was laughing at her!

'You . . . you are a bastard, did you know that?' she

cried, her own voice ragged, but certainly not with held-in chuckles. She was fast becoming furious.

'I have been called that on occasion. And worse. My mother wouldn't be amused,' he replied gravely, but still with that hidden amusement lying just beneath the surface.

'Ooh! Can't you be serious for once?' she demanded. It was impossible to deal with Dane Curtis in this mood, as Helen knew only too well. And yet deal with him she must, or find life truly unbearable living in the same house with him as she was.

'I could, but frankly I think that one of us taking themselves too seriously is enough,' he replied. 'More than enough, if you really want to know.'

'Taking themselves too seriously.' She repeated his words slowly, not really thoughtfully, but enough so that she was forced to react. 'You mean me, obviously. What the hell is that supposed to mean?'

Now he did chuckle, the noise rumbling from his throat in the sound one makes when humouring a fractious child. Helen seethed in silence, waiting for him to speak out, to verbalise whatever he thought was so funny. And when he finally did, she almost wished he hadn't.

'Ah, young Helen, you're thick as two short planks sometimes,' Dane growled finally. 'I think you've been stuck back in the bush too long, for sure. All your journalistic instincts have atrophied and your defence mechanisms are following, from the look of it.'

'How very observant,' she sneered sarcastically. 'And it tells me absolutely nothing.'

'Only because of what I've just said. Really, I'm surprised at you. Not to mention mildly ashamed at seeing you let an amateur like Marina lead you down the garden path like a bull with a ring in its nose. Or have you always been this gullible and I just never noticed before?'

'What *are* you talking about?' Helen cried. 'It's not

me your voluptuous friend led down the garden path. Or any other path, for that matter. It's you—or hadn't you noticed that?'

'Nobody leads me anywhere,' was the stern reply. 'Least of all by using jealousy as their excuse.'

'Jealousy? Who's jealous. And of who?'

'Whom . . . the correct word is whom.'

'Oh, for goodness sake. This is hardly the time to be playing at semantics,' Helen shrieked. 'Can't we even have a discussion without you wanting to correct my grammar while we're at it?'

'We are not having a *discussion*,' Dane smirked. 'We are having, or are about to have, an argument. In fact, I should be very surprised if it doesn't boil up into a full-scale brawl, a proper bloody blue. So I might as well correct your grammar while I'm at it, eh?'

'If you don't stop playing silly beggars and tell me what it is you're getting at, this is going to be more than an argument,' she retorted, blazing now. 'I'm only about thirty seconds away from giving you such a wallop . . .'

'No! Mustn't hit the driver,' he replied. 'Very bad form, that. Drivers have rights; passengers have none.'

'They've got the right to get out and walk, which is just about what I'm tempted to do,' Helen snapped.

'That isn't much of a threat. Unless I stop, which I'm hardly likely to do,' Dane drawled, infuriatingly. 'So let's go back to the original discussion, which, from memory, involved Marina leading you down some path or another. Although you, of course, deny that vehemently.'

'Well of course I do. What she did was lie. L.I.E. Lie. She quite blatantly and deliberately told you that she and I had been discussing Vivian, and you, typically, believed her.'

Dane seemed nonplussed. 'And all of this, I'm sure, followed an equally blatant attempt by Marina to pump you, dear Helen, for information on the subject. Which, knowing you, gained her not very much at all except some intricate footwork and verbal hedging.' And he paused, as if to let that sink in, then continued. 'Because of course your attitude to such questions would be that if she wanted to know, she ought to be asking me, not you. Okay so far?'

She snarled her affirmative reply through gritted teeth, wondering how on earth this man could be so damnably accurate in his guesses. And worse, so damnably smug about being accurate.

'And, of course, she also made a fair bid to find out just what *our* relationship—yours and mine—might be, while she was at it. To which you would have lied or said nothing at all.'

'I did no such thing,' Helen interjected. 'I told her the plain, simple truth . . . that there's nothing at all between us, which, frankly, is exactly what she wanted to hear.'

'Which is the *last* thing she wanted to hear,' Dane corrected. 'Because even if you believed it, there's no possible way Marina could believe it. But . . . it'll keep her on her toes, if nothing else.'

'Which is exactly what you want, isn't it?' Helen suddenly saw what was shaping up; herself as some sort of blonde red herring to keep Marina on her toes and make things easier for Dane to handle as he sorted out his relationship with the redhead. 'That's . . . that's . . . truly despicable,' she sighed. 'If you'd planned on using me for something like that, the least you might have done is told me about it. I thought we were supposed to be friends.'

'Using you for what?' And now she wished he wasn't driving, because it made it only too easy for him to avoid meeting her eyes, made it too easy for him to lie.

'You know damned well what,' she snapped. 'Using me to put your friend Marina off-balance, although how you'd expect me to manage it, I can't imagine.'

'Ah, but I'm not using you for that. Not at all,' he

said, and almost made the denial ring true. 'It wasn't me that bought that dress and gave it life. It wasn't me that arranged for you to be at the party in the first place, and it certainly wasn't me that made Marina foam at the mouth with jealousy. I had nothing to do with it at all.'

'In a pig's eye. If it wasn't for you, she wouldn't give two hoots where I was or what I wore,' Helen replied. 'But of course you already know that.'

'I know that the way you looked tonight in that outfit, every man there was jealous of me,' Dane grinned. 'Most of the women were merely green with envy.' And then he laughed outright. 'Especially Marina, who quite rightfully, I think, blamed you for stealing her thunder. She rather prefers to be belle of the ball, especially at her own parties.'

'Well she's welcome to it,' Helen retorted, her anger only spurred on by the confusion of his compliments. 'Especially if her ego's so fragile that it can only be soothed by you calling me a liar. I'm not a liar and I won't have that sort of thing. Is that perfectly clear?'

'I already told you that I didn't call you a liar; I merely said that you've been known, on occasion, to lie. There's a world of difference.'

'There's not a whit of difference and you know it. What's more, you did it deliberately. And you did it deliberately to spite *her*. That's what offends me. Is that why you brought me down here, to act as some sort of weird buffer between you and your girlfriend?'

'Now really, Helen. Would I do a thing like that?' And his mock indignation was more than Helen could bear. She fairly exploded.

'You could and you bloody well would! And you did! And I won't have it, do you hear me. I won't have it. I won't, damn it!'

But it was to no avail. Dane continued driving as soberly as before, letting the words wash across his broad shoulders like a soft breeze, seemingly oblivious to Helen's anger and hurt and frustration. 'We're nearly home,' he said. 'Let's save the rest of this ... discussion until I can concentrate on it without driving into the ditch or some such silly thing.'

'You can save it forever, for all I care,' Helen snorted. 'I've said all I'm going to say on the subject.'

'Suits me,' Dane replied, turning into the driveway. 'I never wanted to indulge in such a stupid argument in the first place.'

It would have suited Helen as well, except that it kept on nagging at her; even as she was changing before joining Dane for a night-cap, she kept wondering if he could really be using her as some sort of buffer against the obvious attentions of Marina Cole. It was, Helen thought, probably conceited of her to even consider such a thing. She could hardly be considered real competition for such a beautiful and experienced opponent. But the real issue wasn't that at all. It was more closely related to the simple fact of Dane using her in such a fashion. *That* implied a conceit on his part that didn't fit with her own image of Dane, and even worse was the fact that her image was becoming all too important to her, all too real.

He could be so damned charming, only to cut her down like a bad weed at any time she ventured too close to him emotionally. Or ... physically. During the evening, he'd seemed to watch as others danced with her, but hadn't danced with her himself even once. Of course, he'd been rather occupied with their hostess, but still ...

'I'm sorry I seemed to upset you tonight,' he said, handing over a cup of fresh coffee laced with brandy when Helen entered the lounge room wrapped in a long, snuggly towelling robe. 'I suppose I should have realised Marina might decide to take the mickey out of you, and maybe I should have prepared you better.'

'I rather think I'm quite capable of taking care of myself,' Helen replied. Almost coldly, because she still felt she was due an apology far more specific than what he'd offered.

But it was hard to stay angry at him, almost impossible in fact. Leaning casually against a sideboard, his dinner jacket replaced now by a light shaving coat that was only loosely belted at the waist, he looked so . . . unthreatening.

For one wild, heart-fluttering instant, she had the urge to step closer, to trace her fingers through the curls of hair that ran upward from the opening of the robe. Then she caught the gleam in his eye, judged it slightly more mocking than usual, and found her temper returning.

'Well I'm still not happy at you insinuating that I'm a liar,' she declared resolutely.

'Ah . . . that's better,' he grinned. '*Now* all I've done is to insinuate. You're getting nearer to the truth, young Helen, even if you don't want to admit it.'

'And don't call me that,' she snapped. 'Unless you'd prefer that I go around referring to you as grandfather, or some such thing. And I would, no worries.'

'Which would only prove the truth of my . . . insinuations,' he replied, and laughed aloud at her hiss of exasperation. 'Oh no, Helen. I'm no grandfather. I'm no relative at all, except in a sort of weird, second-hand sort of way. And I'm even beginning to wonder about that; you're getting far too mature to need that.'

'Well if I'm so damned mature, will you please stop referring to me as *young Helen*,' she snapped, patience now close to its end. 'Or is it asking too much for you to make up your mind whether I'm too young for . . .' And she stopped, aghast at what she'd almost said.

'Too young for . . . what?' Dane asked, stepping close to her and depositing his coffee cup on the sideboard as he did so. Then he reached out to take Helen's cup from fingers that shook so much they threatened to drop the cup. She didn't see him do it; her eyes were locked on his as he approached, her entire body trembled with something that mingled anticipation with dread.

'No,' she said, but the word was lost in her gasp as his fingers cupped her chin, lifting her eyes, maintaining their lock with his as his face loomed closer.

'Or should I say, for whom?' he asked, voice low and vibrant, pulsing like the movement of blood through her temples. Helen was mute, spellbound by eyes that now were only inches from her own, entranced by the touch of his fingers against her skin, the warmth of his body so close to her.

'No!' Louder, this time. Almost a perceptible whisper, but not, apparently, loud enough for him to hear. Or else he ignored her protest, cutting it off with his own lips so effectively she might as well not have spoken.

Helen shivered as his arms closed around her, but it was a shiver of ecstasy, not of fear. He didn't really need to press her close to him as his lips continued their assault; she was straining against him by herself, her breasts flattening against the hard musculature of his chest, her thighs warmed by the heat of his body.

Only Helen's mind rebelled against his caresses, knowing they were more than just that ... they were the beginnings of a form of punishment, a form of chastisement. And ... it just couldn't be like that. She wanted him, but she wanted him to take her in love, not in punishment, not with the realisation that she would become—almost had already become—a slave in his arms, a captive to his touch, to his kiss.

'No!' And this time he heard; he must have, considering she was forced to wrench free her lips to shout out her denial.

'Yes!' And his lips returned, stifling her objections, bruising against the softness of her mouth even as his strong fingers locked behind her, holding her powerless in his grasp.

No ... no ... no ... but her refusal was no more

than a silent scream as strong arms lifted her, as Dane carried her to the nearby couch.

'Oh, yes, young Helen,' he hissed in her ear as he laid her down, stretching the heat of him, the strength of him, beside her, locking her again in the cradle of his arms. 'I think it's high time we established who's too old—or too young—for whom.'

And now it wasn't only his lips that claimed her; his fingers slid beneath her robe, touching her body with a practised skill, lifting sensation within her as easily as if he were lighting a cigarette. Easier! Only this fire burned strangely, flickering through her sensual regions like a wildfire, touching here and there, almost moving, always striking new fuel. And inside, deep inside the secret centre of her heart, it burned with a fierce, white-hot fury, scorching away common sense, turning logic to ashes.

She couldn't breathe, couldn't think. This was punishment, paradise, love and hatred combined. She wanted him to love her, wanted his body against her like this, his fingers . . . just there. She wanted to use her own hands on a voyage of exploration, then follow with another of her body.

But not like this! Not with him using his skills as a weapon to conquer her, as a rod to punish her. That would take from the love-making everything she needed most.

Everything . . . like his lips at her breast, his tongue a teasing, tantalising sensation against her turgid nipple, like his fingers against the softness of her body, touching, arousing, inflaming, *invading*. Like her own fingers struggling through the hair on his chest, fumbling against the waistband of his slacks, betraying all her logic and reason with a hellish, marvellous abandon.

Until he spoke again. Until he whispered: 'Still think I'm too old?', his voice ragged with desire that seemed to match her own, a voice filled with undertone that

Helen's beleaguered mind interpreted in the only way it could.

He was laughing at her! The impression struck like a thunderbolt, smashing through the lassitude of her near-surrender, lashing at her conscience, her very personal image of herself. And of him.

'Yes!' She spat. The word was acid, smoking lava, smelling of sulphur. Like the boiling inferno of sulphur where her heart had been.

'Yes!' She spat it out again, trying to rid herself of the taste of him. Dane recoiled as if he'd been struck, and Helen sprang up from her position on the couch as if shot from a gun. Her fingers were outstretched like claws; if she touched him now, it would be only to rend, to tear away the smugness and the conceit.

He reached out, but halted the gesture when she flashed her nails at him like a fist full of swords. 'What's wrong?' he asked, and for an instant she could almost believe the expression of bewilderment in his eyes. But only for an instant; she knew better, deep inside.

'You . . . you utter bastard!' she cried, reaching out in her anger, her rage. 'You know what's wrong . . . you *made* it wrong.'

'No, Helen,' he replied, voice soft, still bemused but now regaining the total control she would have expected. 'No, I don't, and I didn't.'

'You did! Damn it, you *did*! Look at us. This could have been and should have been something beautiful, not some sort of *let's get Helen under control*. You . . . you just don't understand.'

And that was the crux of it, she knew. Even if he were honest, he didn't understand and could never and never would.

'I certainly never thought of it as anything like that,' he said, voice now velvet-smooth, controlled.

'You never thought of it as anything at all,' Helen snapped, 'because you don't think. You just manipulate, using people like puppets to suit your own selfish ends. You manipulated me to help you manipulate Marina Cole, and probably the other way round as well. People aren't real, to you. They're just like the characters in your damned books. Well . . . not me. Not anymore.'

'What we were just doing, Helen, was not exactly the sort of manipulation you're talking about,' Dane replied softly, but to Helen there was an underlying anger in his voice. There must be, after the accusation she'd just flung at him.

'Like hell,' she cried. 'It was exactly the kind of manipulation I was talking about. Is that what you do with Marina when she argues? Stop talking and whirl her into bed where you can control her? Is that what you did with Vivian?'

And then she paused, her voice stilled by the unholy light that sprang like lightning from Dane's eyes. His jaw clenched, the muscles in his neck tautened, she could almost hear his teeth grinding together as he fought for control.

No question—she'd done the unforgivable. Done it without thinking, without even vaguely considering the consequences. But she'd done it, and now she felt fear . . . very real fear.

Dane leaned towards her, his eyes blazing, his fists clenched at his sides. He loomed like some enormous spectre, some monster out of imagination, but he didn't touch her. Yet.

'I . . . I . . . oh, God, I'm sorry,' Helen stammered. 'Please, Dane. I didn't mean to say that, or even think it. Honestly.' And as she spoke, she was already involved in a steady retreat towards the hallway and the door to her room, for what questionable safety that might offer.

He didn't reply . . . and he didn't follow.

CHAPTER SIX

HELEN barely slept that night, at first because she was half-convinced that Dane eventually would follow her, that some physical punishment was unavoidable. And then because she found herself forced to try and sort out her own position, a position that seemed increasingly more precarious.

But ... what to do? She still had no money, no job, nowhere to go. In truth, she didn't even want to go; she wanted to stay and no longer bothered to try and deny that to herself. But not this way, not with Dane angry at her, perhaps even hating her. And not with herself in such a vulnerable position, feeling as she did about a man who couldn't return her love.

Long before the sun rose, Helen was wide awake, her eyes smarting from straining through the classified sections of every weekend paper they'd bought the day before. By breakfast time, she'd already done almost a full day's work; there were six completed job applications neatly stacked in front of her.

She'd had to force herself to ignore the fact that she wasn't qualified enough for two of them, was probably over-qualified for another two, and wasn't professionally interested in either of the remaining two. Personally, yes, but not professionally.

'But it doesn't matter. Any of them will give me a way out,' she sighed. And a way out was what she now needed. Desperately. Even, she thought, if it meant moving to Melbourne or Adelaide or even—perish the thought—Sydney. Even if it meant taking a job that would bore her stupid within three weeks.

The worst problem was that even the application deadlines were at least a week away; it could be a

month before all but one of the positions was filled.
And in the meantime . . .?

'The world could come to an end in the meantime,'
she muttered to herself.

'It could come to an end tomorrow, but I wouldn't
lose any sleep over it,' said an unexpectedly pleasant
voice behind her. 'You, on the other hand, look as if
you've lost plenty,' Dane said as Helen turned to face
him, unsure of whether he mightn't still be angry.

'Jobs?' he asked, no trace of last night's unpleasant-
ness in his voice, but certainly not with a smile, either.

'I . . . I really think it's about time,' Helen replied,
hardly able to meet his gaze.

'Because of last night? Or just generally?' Damn him
for his directness, she thought, a faint blush riding up
through the neckline of her robe at his abrupt
questions.

'A bit of both, I suppose,' she replied, trying to keep
her voice casual, trying not to make too much out of it.

'Humph! How much of each, I wonder,' he grunted.
'And don't bother to answer that. Just let me say that I
hope it's only a little bit because of last night. Okay, so
we had a bit of a blue. People do, you know. Even the
most happily . . . ah . . . the best adjusted people do,
sometimes. It sort of goes with the territory. Hell, even
Vivian and I had the occasional fight.'

Helen winced at his use of the name, at the direct link
between this morning's relatively civilised discussion
and the abuse-laden atmosphere of the night before.
But she couldn't answer him, didn't dare to try and put
into words the way she felt. Not now.

Striding over to the kitchen counter, Dane poured
each of them a cup of coffee, idly humming to himself
as he did so. Then he placed the cups on the table and
slid into a chair opposite Helen.

Lean, tanned fingers reached out to pick up the stack
of advertisements, leafing through them as if they were
a pack of cards. Helen watched not the hands, but the

face of the man who now studied the possible basis of her future plans.

'Rather scraping the bottom of the barrel in places,' he muttered, lifting his head to search Helen's face intently. 'I thought you weren't rapt in big cities.'

'I'm not rapt in being unemployed forever, either,' she replied. A bit cockily, considering the circumstances. Dane grinned in recognition of her attitude.

'Being a jillaroo isn't exactly the same as being unemployed,' he smiled. 'Even if it does pay about the same.'

'That isn't the issue,' Helen replied, lying just a little. It *was* the issue, at least in part. She wasn't a jillaroo, not really. She wasn't, in truth, anything at all. She had no status but that of a visitor, no matter how Dane thought of her. No longer able even to think of him as a surrogate brother, she found it equally impossible to think of herself as either housekeeper, jillaroo, executive assistant, cook, or anything else. Except perhaps his wife and lover—but Helen's standards made her want both roles combined; to be only his lover would be too hurtful, and quite impossible if he were to marry again.

Especially, she thought, if he were to marry Marina Cole. Then her own thoughts were interrupted by that too-familiar voice.

'I've just thought of one solution, and have to admit I'm due a licking for not having thought of it sooner,' Dane was saying. 'We should have put you on the casual list as soon as you got here, and I should damned well have thought of it. And so should you.'

'So I should,' Helen admitted, admitting silently to herself that it might have been the ideal solution when she first arrived, but not any more, not permanently. Still, the Australian Journalists' Association casual list could provide work, perhaps even immediate work, and the temporary nature was no longer an issue.

'No sooner said than done,' Dane grinned. 'I'm seeing the AJA secretary at this meeting I have to attend

today, so I'll take care of it for you. And,' picking up
the stack of applications, 'I'll drop these in the mail for
you while I'm at it.'

'Meetings on a Sunday?' Helen asked the question
without even considering she might be being rudely
inquisitive. Dane obviously didn't think so either,
because he explained in some detail the information he
was seeking and the need for a weekend meeting to get
all the required people together at once.

'And what are you going to do with yourself?' he
asked then, making the question sound as if he had
something specific he wanted her to do.

'I thought I'd see if Joshua is going to accept
backing,' Helen replied. 'He's really settled down a lot,
and doesn't seem to mind the saddle and all. And it's a
nice day for it; not too much wind to make him all
spooky.'

And she had to grin. It was still a source of great
humour to her the way donkeys seemed to go all
strange on windy days, running and kicking up their
heels as if they were ridden by fairies, or driven by some
elemental magic no human could see.

Dane, however, didn't grin. 'And if he dumps you off
on your pretty little head, with nobody about to pick
you up? No, I think I'd prefer you waited until a day
when I can be here.'

'Oh, for goodness sake,' Helen replied. 'I've been
bounced off horses before. Plenty of times. And apart
from a minor scar or two I'm still here.'

'Well we don't need any more scars,' he replied
grimly. 'How am I to concentrate on my meeting if I
have to be worrying about you all the way through it?'

'Very flattering, but hardly necessary,' Helen scoffed.
'That is one place I don't need anybody worrying about
me.'

'That's not the point and you know it,' he scowled.
And was about to say something else when Helen
interrupted.

'It's exactly the point. Especially if any of these jobs comes up, or something casual is going. Joshua is coming along splendidly, but he needs that bit of work every day. I'm damned if I'm going to leave here with that job half-done, and all my effort wasted.'

'Well just be damned well careful, that's all.' And there was a rising note in his voice, a note that said this could easily become more than a tiny disagreement. Helen didn't have the heart for another fight, not now that they seemed to have cooled down after last night's blue.

'Oh, I suppose one more day won't matter,' she muttered, gulping down the rest of her coffee. It wasn't a promise, but it might sound like one to him, especially if she managed to change the subject quickly and thoroughly enough. The clock helped, there. 'And now you'd best get organised, or you'll be late for your meeting,' she advised. 'Do you want me to whip up some breakfast while you're getting ready?'

He didn't, and indeed was out of the house fifteen minutes later, leaving Helen with the option of going back to bed if she chose. It was tempting, too, having barely slept during the night, but not quite tempting enough.

Her mind was too busy, for one thing. Busy trying to relate Dane's concerned attitude this morning with his anger of the night before, with his arrogant seduction attempt, and with her own responses.

Especially, she thought, her own responses. Had Dane Curtis begun making love to her this morning, in a mood of protectiveness instead of dissension, she had little doubt of the outcome. And that worried her; she was simply too vulnerable, had too few defences against her own depth of feeling and his undeniable charm.

'And worrying about it like this isn't going to help, not one little bit,' she declared savagely. 'I've done what I can, for the moment, and maybe now I should start thinking constructively and stop spinning my wheels.'

A few minutes later she was in the small yards, speaking soothing baby-talk to Joshua as she ran the dandy brush across his gleaming chocolate coat, then picked up his feet for cleaning, working him slowly and deliberately through the already-learned activities leading up to actually climbing into the Indian military saddle.

Molly frisked about at their feet, and although Joshua now appeared scarcely watchful of the dog, Helen made a mental notation to go put Molly in the yard before she actually attempted to get on the donkey's back. The big chocolate gelding was being so completely biddable that Dane's warning was—if not forgotten—then thrust far back out of the way. Today should be the day, Helen thought. The weather was right; she was just in the mood for such an adventure; and Joshua himself seemed to be in the mood as well, which might be the most important consideration.

But first, Molly must be confined. It was only sensible, and they were halfway back to the house when the black dog suddenly dashed ahead, barking her warnings loudly at the sleek sedan that was cruising up the driveway.

Helen was mystified at first, then smiled as she recognised the tall young man who emerged from the vehicle. 'It's Geoff, isn't it? Geoff . . . Jones.'

'It is, and I'm glad I wasn't forgotten in the pack,' he replied with a grin she remembered quite well from the evening before. He'd been quite the nicest of the young men who'd shown a definite interest in the Helen Fredericks of Victorian dress, and from the look in his eye he wasn't averse to the blue-jean-and-jumper-version, either.

Tall, blond and almost too good looking, he stood looking down at her with bold, yet cautious, admiration.

'Dane isn't here just now,' Helen said, suddenly thinking that she was being a bit conceited to think immediately that might be herself that was the attraction. She'd noticed Geoff and Dane in conversation at one point during the party; they obviously knew one another.

'Just as well, since it isn't Dane I've come to see,' was the immediately relieving reply. 'I was actually looking for a rather mysterious blonde in an old-fashioned dress. I don't suppose you've seen anyone like that about?' Geoff grinned. 'Be very hard to miss, I'd expect. Very beautiful, gorgeous grey eyes.'

Helen looked down at her riding gear, then shook her head with a grin of her own. 'Sounds to me like a Cinderella type,' she laughed. 'Probably turned into a pumpkin at midnight. You've not got a glass slipper, by any chance?'

'And I'm not a prince, either,' Geoff smiled with a shake of his head. 'Ah well, if she's not here perhaps I can persuade *you* to join me for lunch.'

'Dressed like this? I should certainly hope not,' Helen scoffed.

'Well we do have plenty of time,' was the reply. 'Unless of course you're really otherwise engaged, or too busy or something.'

Helen couldn't help herself. 'That's the problem,' she said seriously. 'I have this date with a bloke called Joshua, you see. And it's something we've been working up to for quite a long time; I'm not sure I ought to break it.'

'But you . . . might be persuaded?'

Full marks for persistence, she thought, and then chided herself for being uncharitable. She quite liked Geoff, and perhaps it wasn't fair to tease him quite so thoroughly.

He was too young, at least in some ways, but he was good fun, and someone she could talk to without inhibitions or problems. Pleasant company, and today that might be just the ticket!

'Actually, I think it might be better to get my

appointment with Joshua out of the way first,' Helen said with a grin. 'And having you here might make it a bit easier, actually, considering I had sort of promised I wouldn't try to cope with him alone. Do you ride?'

'But of course. I am, with modesty, not a bad rider at all,' Geoff replied. And laughed pleasantly when Helen then explained about Joshua and her vague promise to Dane. 'I do have to say that I've never ridden on a donkey,' Geoff said. 'But Dane was right, I expect, and I'm very glad indeed to be on hand just in case. Try not to fall off, though, because I'm certain you'd be the type to insist on climbing right back on again, which would eventually make us late for lunch.'

Helen laughed, promised lightly to be as careful as she could, and boosted herself into the saddle with renewed confidence, knowing Geoff had a good hold on the headstall. Joshua, almost to her disappointment, ignored her entirely. He was perfectly happy to walk slowly around the yards, first with Geoff leading and then with Helen guiding him through the reins. Five minutes, no more, and the last big hurdle was well-and-truly over. Joshua was now well on the way to being a proper riding donkey.

'You've certainly schooled him well,' Geoff complimented as they stowed away the gear and walked towards the house. 'I'd have expected a lot more action than that.'

'If he'd been a horse. Donkeys are much smarter,' Helen said. 'But I am pleased; it shows I did a good job from the beginning. Now, can I get you a drink to occupy you while I have a shower and change?'

'Unless you'd rather I came along to scrub your back,' he prompted, with a grin that suggested he didn't expect her to take the suggestion seriously but wouldn't mind if she did.

Helen laughed silently. 'That might be setting your sights a bit high,' she replied. 'Which is what happened to Joshua, and look what it got him.'

Geoff shrugged. 'I can think of few things nicer than being taken in hand by an expert horsewoman like you,' he said.

'Oh, but it would mean being gelded, too,' Helen replied, and giggled as he blanched at the reply, then hastily withdrew his comment.

'On second thoughts, I'll settle for a scotch-and-soda. Shall I have something ready for you when you're ready?'

'Only if you can manage vodka-lime-and-soda,' Helen replied over her shoulder as she exited. 'I won't be more than five minutes.'

Actually, it was closer to ten minutes when she returned, now clothed in a light, casual dress, low-heeled sandals, and a cardigan in case the afternoon turned cool.

Geoff handed her a drink and shot her an admiring glance. 'After your parting shot, I'm almost afraid to say it, but you look lovely,' he said cautiously, and Helen smiled.

'Even I know the difference between flattery and rude suggestions,' she said. 'So . . . thank you. Now . . . what about this luncheon plan? I have to admit I'm about ready for it; I didn't get round to breakfast this morning.'

'Well that, at least, I can fix,' he grinned, obviously having shrugged off her earlier rejection without trauma. 'Drink up and start thinking about the finest of seafoods; it isn't far from here.

Nor was it. Fifteen minutes later they were seated in the wood-panelled lounge of the Oyster Cove Inn, at Kettering, looking across the D'Entrecasteaux Channel at Bruny Island and debating the relative merits of the blackboard menu.

'I can recommend any of it,' Geoff was saying, 'but especially the squid rings and the scallops, of course. And when we're done, I suggest a trek right round through the Huon, if you've never seen it.'

'When we're done, it'll be time to go home, judging from the size of the servings,' Helen whispered. 'Lord, these people must have hollow legs.' And she looked apprehensively around her at the heaping platters of choice seafood that were being distributed to other tables.

But at Geoff's encouraging, she finally settled on squid rings to start, followed by scallops. Tasmanian scallops, she was finding much to her delight, were tastier and sweeter than those in Queensland; she couldn't possibly pass them up.

'I know I asked you this last night, but are you really just a surrogate kid sister to Dane?' Geoff had waited until the food arrived before slinging that question, and Helen nearly choked on a piece of squid as she fumbled for a reply that hovered between honesty and truth.

'Always have been, as long as I've known him,' she replied finally. Truth, if not exactly honesty. All she could do now was hope Geoff would accept the answer; she didn't want to get involved in lengthy explanations now, even if she could manage them.

'And he's not all that old,' she added, hoping to jar his thinking away from the original question. 'How old are you?'

'Exactly the right age for you, or at least that's what I would have said before you got so vehement about donkey operations,' he grinned. 'Actually, I'm thirty-two.'

'Which isn't all that much younger than Dane,' Helen said. Lying, because even if their actual years had been reversed, Geoff would have been the younger. He lacked the maturity, the old-wine quality, wasn't as mature as Dane had been at the same age, much less now.

She looked away, feeling slightly guilty. What was she doing here, she wondered, and then relaxed again with the assurance of her mind that being with Geoff meant nothing but an uncomplicated and pleasant afternoon. She could handle Geoff; already had, once.

She sat back to enjoy the rest of her lunch, idly following Geoff's conversation but no longer terribly interested in him. He was, she decided, too easy to handle; she'd be lucky to get through the rest of the afternoon without being bored.

Dane, on the other hand, was never boring. And, she decided, never the type she could handle easily, if at all. He was just too confident, too much his own person, and too totally unpredictable to be taken as casually for granted as she could Geoff.

Still, it was pleasant to be courted without threat, to be wined and dined and driven on what turned out to be a marvellously scenic expedition around the exterior of the Huon peninsula. With the channel on their left, they drove south through Woodbridge and Middleton and Gordon, then swung westward across the bottom of the peninsula through to Garden Island Creek, then northward along the estuary of the Huon River, through the orchard country, the gently rolling hillsides covered in apple and small fruit orchards. And finally, back eastward again across the high passes of the upper Huon, back to the highway leading home.

Geoff, obviously slightly disappointed at not having been able to persuade Helen to stay with him for the evening as well, didn't come in for a drink, although he brightened considerably when she thanked him for the afternoon with a kiss on the cheek.

'We must arrange to do something like this again,' he said, and Helen politely agreed despite knowing she would endeavour to be sure of being too busy, in future. He was a nice boy, but only in small doses, she decided.

Dane, as predicted, still wasn't home, so Helen changed and spent the next hour feeding the livestock and doing some training with Molly. The 142-kilometre round-trip drive had done nothing to help wear off the enormous lunch, and Helen rightly felt the need for some exercise if she was to be expected to eat dinner as well that day.

As it turned out, she didn't have to worry. Dane phoned a few minutes after she returned to the house, announcing he'd be back later than he'd expected and asking if she'd mind feeding the stock for him. Helen was pleased and gratified at his obvious pleasure when she announced those chores were already taken care of, but the highlight of her day didn't occur until he'd personally returned home with news.

'I've arranged you a casual sub-editor's job at the *Mercury* for a couple of weeks,' he said after sprawling in his usual chair with a mild Scotch in his hand. 'The money's no good and the hours are terrible, but at least it'll get you out into the wide world again.'

'Thank you, although you don't have to sound so pleased to get rid of me,' Helen replied.

'Nobody's trying to get rid of you; this was your own idea,' he growled. 'And damned well remember that when the four-to-midnight shift starts getting you down.'

'Actually, I've never minded that shift,' she replied honestly. 'One can still get a reasonable sleep and have time to sunbathe all day, or whatever.'

'Ah ... and is that what you were up to today? I called a couple of times, but you were obviously outside.'

'More than just outside,' she said, ignoring her earlier decision not to mention her excursion. 'I've been taken all over the place; lunch at the Oyster Cove Inn, and then a trek all round the Huon, playing tourist.'

And as she spoke, Helen watched him, seeking some sign of interest, or ... she didn't know what. Which was why she paused rather dramatically before announcing, 'With Geoff Jones.'

But if she expected—had she? to see any sign of jealousy on Dane's rugged features, she was not surprisingly disappointed. 'Ah,' he said. 'Young Geoff's pretty quick off the mark, but then that's his style, and it seems to work for him as often as not.' Dane leaned back in his chair, pausing long enough to light a cigarette.

There was an expression in his eye now that Helen definitely didn't like; it didn't quite accuse, but she detected a hint of insinuation there somewhere.

'And just what is that supposed to mean?' she demanded, sending him a stern glance along with the question.

'In your case? I'd be amazed—indeed astounded—if it meant anything at all,' was the surprising reply. 'You might have ended up bored stupid after an afternoon with him, but I really can't imagine you ending up in bed.'

It was so damnably accurate that Helen gasped, openly. Then sat there with her mouth open for an instant as she tried to think of a suitable reply. It was frightening, almost annoying, to have this man so easily able to predict her reactions, almost to read her mind.

'He's ... he's very handsome, though,' she finally said. A silly statement and she knew it. What was she trying to do ... deliberately make Dane jealous? If so, she wasn't doing much of a job of it.

'So's Joshua,' Dane said then, very quietly, very soberly, but with a twinkle in his eye.

And Helen broke up. She fairly rolled out of her chair with almost hysterical laughter in memory of her earlier comment to Geoff, and his reaction, and Dane's perplexed expression at her own reactions to what must have seemed a rather innocuous comment.

It was minutes before she could stop laughing, before she could stifle the bubbling chuckles long enough to gasp out a reply to his, 'I really can't see why it's all that funny.'

And Dane, of course, didn't laugh as much as she had when it was explained to him. Just enough, Helen thought, to show his appreciation of her own wit, her ability to keep someone like Geoff in his place.

'After your reception by the younger set last night, I'd been thinking I might have to sit out on the porch at night with a shotgun,' he finally said. 'But I reckon you can handle yourself without my help.'

'Especially since I won't be here at night,' Helen replied with exaggerated haughtiness. 'Which is just as well, because if I had to think of you in such ludicrous circumstances, it might make it difficult to handle anything. I'd be too busy laughing to defend myself.'

Which wasn't quite true, she decided after retiring to the warmth of her bed. There was something rather . . . comforting about the thought of Dane protecting her. Something tender and very, very welcome. Except that it was probably only something of a dream in the first place. His brother-figure image might still be alive in his mind, but in her own it was long since vanquished by another image, far less brotherly but far more welcome should it decide to investigate reality.

And during the next few days, he played neither role, but instead buried himself in his office. Helen spent most of each day with Joshua, who seemed now to have fully accepted her control and even went so far as to begin greeting his saddling each day with some enthusiasm.

Finally, however, it was time to take on the casual job Dane had arranged, and Helen quickly found that she'd unintentionally lied about enjoying the four to midnight shift. Or rather, she thought after the first three days, not the shift so much as the day-to-day routine. She could handle the work standing on her head, but she quickly found that her day began not with the beginning of work, but at the end of it. Returning home in the dark, silent hours, she found it difficult to sleep, and usually didn't drift off until nearly dawn. She saw virtually nothing of Dane, who was usually asleep—or at least pretending to be—by the time she got home, and was ensconced in his office throughout each day.

Their conversation at lunch, on those days when he bothered to eat, was usually confined to trivialities like her work, and she could tell without being told that he was into the home stretch of his latest novel, his mind fully engrossed on the work.

Her mind, on the other hand, seemed to have far too much scope in which to roam. So much so that she spent three afternoons working out the kitchen plans he'd asked for, although she had to force herself to remind herself that this wasn't going to be *her* kitchen, but somebody else's . . . probably Marina Cole's.

Twice during the fortnight's casual work, Helen found herself editing catch-lines for social pictures in which the elegant brunette featured. One of them had Dane, as well, and she had to look up quickly to see if the editor who'd passed it to her was deliberately seeking some reaction. Apparently not, or else she'd not been quick enough.

She looked at the picture critically, scolding herself for the instant pangs of jealousy it created. Unfounded jealousy, even, because the information given her with the picture made it clear that Dane and Marina had been separately invited to the affair at which the photo had been taken.

But what really hurt was that he hadn't so much as mentioned to Helen that he'd been invited in the first place. Nor that he was going. Fair enough that she would have been working and thus unable to join him, but still . . .

And then she laughed at herself. Quietly, almost scornfully. What possible right did she have to criticise Dane's movements or the company he chose? She was no more than a guest in his house, which meant he was certainly under no obligation to explain to her. Except . . . he usually did. Thinking back, Helen couldn't remember another occasion when he'd neglected to tell her he was going to be out. So why this time?

The answer, she thought, was very likely smiling at

her out of the picture, revealing perfect teeth in an expression that seemed to be directed specifically at Helen herself. A sort of gloating look, she decided, and chuckled at her immediate instinct to stick out her tongue in response.

'Definitely catty,' she muttered, glancing hastily over her shoulder to see if anybody'd noticed. Then she got busy and wrote the required catch-lines, as if by doing the job quickly she could dispense with her thoughts as easily as she did the picture.

And as she drove homeward after work, driving Dane's car to Dane's house, she sturdily resolved not to mention the picture unless he brought up the subject himself.

Which, surprisingly, he didn't. Not even when he read the paper over breakfast, with Helen sitting squarely across the table from him, knowing he must see the picture, knowing he couldn't possibly miss it.

Helen had felt her anticipation building from the moment he'd picked up the newspaper, and she felt almost giddy with surprise as she watched his eyes skim through the news columns, saw his fingers turn page after page until he'd reached, and finally passed, the one with the picture prominently displayed.

She kept watching him, almost willing him to say something, but when he'd finished reading, his only comment was to ask if she'd like more coffee.

'You finish up tonight, I gather,' he said after returning to the table. 'Anything else on offer, or is this the end of it for now?'

'It's the end unless one of those applications comes good,' Helen replied. 'Why? Do you have something specific you want me to do?'

'Not really. I was just sort of thinking that we might go to dinner tomorrow night and celebrate, provided of course I get this damned book done by then.'

'That *would* be something to celebrate,' Helen cried. 'But I didn't realise you were that close to finishing.'

'Nothing but sheer talent,' he grinned, 'although I must admit to being slightly surprised myself. These last few weeks have been excellent from a concentration point of view, and the thing really took off.'

'Is that a subtle hint that I should go find another job quickly so you can get started on your next epic?' The words were out before she thought of their impact, but Dane didn't seem to notice the waspish tone.

'More the opposite, if anything,' he replied. 'I wasn't just thinking of the fortnight you've been working, but of the whole time you've been here.'

'That sounds almost like a compliment,' she smiled.

'That *is* a compliment. But don't rush around getting a swelled head about it. What I really want you to do is make a decision about where you're taking me for dinner.'

Helen paused. 'Where I'm taking you for dinner? Haven't you got it backwards? A minute ago I got the distinct impression that you were inviting me.'

'Semantics. Always semantics,' he replied with a Cheshire-cat grin. 'A minute ago I said that *we* should go to dinner to celebrate the end of your job and the end of my book. Now what I'm about to discuss is where we're going. The question of who pays is already settled because you're the one who'll get paid tonight; I don't get paid until my book's published.'

'And with my luck, you'd decide you want to dine at the casino, which will devour my entire pay cheque,' Helen muttered half to herself. Not that she begrudged the expenditure, but she had been hoping to save as much of her pay as possible to expedite her departure. Only she couldn't tell him that.

'What an excellent suggestion.' She might have known he'd say that; he'd been half-promising for weeks to make the revolving restaurant atop the Wrest Point casino the venue for their next dining adventure.

'Someday I'll learn to keep my mouth shut,' Helen snorted, forgetting entirely that the original intent of his comments had been for *her* to choose. Then she remembered, but didn't even bother to mention that little fact. It was too late.

'Well you don't want to start tomorrow night,' Dane replied with a victorious grin. 'The tucker at the casino is usually first-rate and even a cynic like me has to admit that the view is worth the price of the dinner anyway.'

He went on to rhapsodise about such dishes as he remembered, predictably stressing the various *game* dishes, including venison medallions and hare in port, but Helen did her best to tune out the images which appeared in her own mind with dollar signs attached.

'We'll go early, I think, and maybe we can manage to win enough at two-up, or roulette to pay for dinner,' he continued.

'With my luck? Oh, no. I'm not about to risk my hard-earned cash that way.' Helen was adamant; gambling was something for which she had little interest, bar the occasional lottery ticket. 'But certainly we can go early if you like,' she continued. 'I've got no objection at all to standing around being decorative while your throw *your* money away.'

'And reminding me when I win that I'll be expected to pay for dinner myself? I'll just bet you would too,' was the reply.

'Well I don't know why not. After all, if my presence brings you the luck, surely I'm entitled to some reward.' She was smiling now, comfortable in the renewal of their old bantering relationship, able to shrug off the trauma of the other, less pleasant times.

Dane chuckled. 'If it wasn't for the fact that all the black-jack dealers there are women, I'd be inclined to take you up on that,' he said. 'With men dealing, I'd rig you out in that fancy old-fashioned gown and totally destroy their concentration.'

Helen grinned in reply. 'Goodness, two compliments in the same day and we've barely finished breakfast. I think I'll have to watch out; you're never this complimentary unless you're up to something funny.'

'Nothing funny about it. I was merely providing a subtle suggestion in hopes you'd remember it when it comes time to choose what you'll wear tomorrow night. I quite like that dress; it's the most flattering thing I think you've worn.'

And his tone was serious. Not heavily so, but enough that Helen was momentarily stuck for a reply. Dane wasn't given to idle compliments, and she found herself revelling in his praise.

'Certainly I'll wear it if that's what you'd like,' she finally said, surprised to find herself also slightly embarrassed by his compliment. 'I . . . I rather fancied the way it came out, myself.'

'And so you should.' He threw that comment over his shoulder as he left the room, obviously heading for his office and the final work on his book.

Helen, preparing for their dinner date the next afternoon, found Dane's compliments echoing in her mind as she primped, and was glad she hadn't followed through with a vague notion the week before to have her hair re-styled. Short, it would have been more convenient, but impossible to pile high to create the right effect to match her gown.

She'd spent a bit of her fortnight's pay packet on some new make-up, which she applied judiciously, ever-mindful of the adage that the proper way to wear make-up was so that it created a totally natural effect. With this gown, especially, the natural look was vital, she thought, adding in her mind the knowledge that Dane did not like excessive make-up, then pondering the logic of his attraction to Marina Cole, who in Helen's opinion, wasted a gorgeous complexion by covering it with make-up.

Then she shook her head vigorously, nearly dislodging the half-completed hair-do. No, she would not think about Marina Cole. Not tonight, and hopefully never again. Although perhaps that was expecting too much, Helen decided. But not tonight, at least.

Tonight, she would think only pleasant thoughts about pleasant things. Like a gourmet dinner, even if she *was* paying for it ... like the pleasure of Dane's company with herself looking her best. Perhaps she would even have a bit of a flutter at the gaming tables, see if her luck was—finally—changing. Just a bit of a flutter, and that, she thought, after dinner. Maybe she'd win, although on past performance it didn't seem likely.

Still, tonight she felt lucky, somehow. And it was a feeling enhanced when she finally emerged to an approving look from her escort, a smile, and the comment that she looked 'just perfect'.

Dane, resplendent himself in evening wear, seemed especially solicitous as he handed her into the car, then out again in the casino parking lot.

Looking up at the massive, cylindrical structure, lights ablaze, Helen could almost *feel* the excitement being generated by the crowds already gathered in the gaming rooms. Her arm linked through Dane's, she stood for a moment as if gathering her breath, drinking in the aura of expectancy before they walked together through the glittering, circular entryway.

Inside the lobby with its ultra-modern decor and vivid colours, the air of excitement and expectancy became distinctly tangible. People were everywhere, all of them seemingly moving in a purposeful manner, usually towards the gaming tables in rooms to the right of the entrance.

'Well, do we have a flutter now, or wait until after dinner?' Dane asked. 'We're a bit early for our dinner booking, but if you'd rather not gamble we can just be sight-seers, like most of the others here.'

Helen hesitated, then decided on a visit to the gaming rooms. She'd set aside ten dollars, determined not to risk a single cent more regardless of temptation.

After exchanging the money for chips, as did Dane

with an incredibly large amount, Helen allowed herself to be guided on a tour of the gaming rooms, where crowds jammed in around the attractions of Black Jack, Roulette, Punto Blanco and Craps. Further along, the largest crowd of all was urging along the uniquely Australian 'two-up' game, in which two coins were flipped into the air from a specially-prepared board held by the 'spinner'.

'I've never tried roulette,' she admitted, and after some consultation left Dane to slide into a chair that became vacant at one of the blackjack tables while she wandered over to the roulette wheel.

Twenty minutes later—twenty incredibly fast-moving minutes in which astonishment combined with confusion and excitement to leave her almost reeling—Helen was ninety dollars richer and nearly faint from disbelief.

And a few moments later she was standing in the crowd behind Dane's blackjack table, her small evening bag jammed with chips and her heart still racing madly. When he finally left the table and moved up to join her, she was flushed and bright-eyed, still not sure she dared believe it had all really happened.

'It's like a dream,' she said, showing him the winnings. 'It just seemed like every bet I made simply had to win.'

'Except for the last one?' And his smile was tinged with a vague expression of wry amusement.

'Oh no. Every one. I never lost once.'

'And yet you quit playing? You'll never make a gambler, dear Helen. It's one thing to quit while you're ahead, but to walk out in the middle of a winning streak . . .'

'I don't think it's at all unreasonable.' She was feeling mildly defensive and his amused attitude didn't help.

'It isn't. Just interesting,' he smiled. 'Although, it does make me wonder if you're not growing up to be a shade *too* cautious. I'd have expected that once you started winning you'd have tried to keep at least a small portion of your winnings going, just to try and keep the winning streak alive.'

'Of course that's what you'd have done?' Helen wasn't angry, just mildly bewildered by his attitude. What possible difference could it make anyway?

'But of course. Winning streaks happen so rarely in one's life that keeping them going is almost a duty.'

'Yes. Well I'm afraid I was so excited and then so . . . well, frightened. Money shouldn't come that easily. So I got scared and quit before I got in deeper than I wanted to.' Helen paused, suddenly aware for an instant of the throngs around them. 'I suppose you'd call that silly?'

Dane's gaze was serious; he wasn't laughing at her and he wasn't going to provide a frivolous answer, she realised. 'No, I'd call it sensible,' he said. 'Most girls I know would have plunged in willy-nilly and probably ended up losing the lot. But then, you're not *most girls*, are you dear Helen?'

There was no safe reply to that, so she didn't bother to try, and a moment later it was Dane who continued.

'At any rate, it appears you've won enough to pay for dinner without a qualm, so let's trot along and see what goodies they have upstairs, shall we?'

And moments later they were rising seventeen floors up in the lift, to emerge in a small lobby where a tank of live, enormous crayfish moved turgidly about while waiting to become someone's dinner.

The restaurant itself was an almost breathtaking creation of red plush and chrome, and even it was overshadowed by the magnificence of the view it afforded. As they were escorted to their table, Helen found herself allowing Dane to guide her with one hand on her arm; her own eyes were drawn to the windows through which the lights of the city and the surrounding region seemed to come alive.

Dane explained after they were seated that the dining portion of the restaurant was a vast wheel, revolving once every ninety minutes around the stationary centre which contained the kitchens, the lift and the restrooms.

'All very fancy gadgetry, but it certainly provides the desired effect,' he chuckled. 'And what's more important, the food usually lives up to the expectations created by such a stunning setting.'

The casino was located in Sandy Bay, south of the city proper, and the view as the restaurant revolved ranged from the blackness of the sea to the southeast along the Derwent estuary around to take in the hills and valleys of the night-lit city, then the river and the fairy span of the Tasman Bridge, with the newer Bowen Bridge further upstream.

However beautiful, it was all confusing to Helen's eyes, but Dane patiently explained the various sights as their meal arrived course by course and the view revolved beneath them in a panorama of inky blackness and twinkling lights.

By the time their table had made one complete revolution, the combination of excellent food, the stunning view and copious helpings of the dinner wine had brought Helen to a state of flushed, expectant excitement. Her evening was going so perfectly, she thought, that it was becoming something of a dream, a vision to be remembered forever.

And then Marina Cole stepped into the dream, shattering it into a million crystal shards.

CHAPTER SEVEN

'DARLING!' Marina's smouldering eyes touched both of them, but Helen knew the greeting was for Dane alone. And as the brunette strode forward, arms outstretched towards the man who rose to meet her, Helen wished she could somehow drop through a hole in the floor, anything, just so that she could disappear.

'But what a marvellous surprise,' Marina crooned as she slid into the empty chair beside Dane, who seated himself only after Marina herself. 'What ever are you doing here? I thought you were still hibernating with your latest novel or something.'

'I was. But now we're celebrating the end of it, among other things,' Dane replied with a smile, and Helen felt herself cringe at the warmth of it.

Damn the woman, Helen thought. Damn, and double-damn. How could she stroll in here so blithely, so confidently, and so thoroughly destroy an entire evening just like that? It was just so ... so frustrating. And the more so because she could do nothing about it; only sit silently and listen to the silken voice that addressed Dane like some lewd caress.

'You've finished it? Oh, how marvellous for you,' said Marina in gushing tones that seemed to Helen to be almost glutinous. 'But what's this other thing you're celebrating? Oh, it's just so exciting. I shall have to order us all champagne, I think.'

For which read, Dane will have to order it. And I'll have to pay for it, probably, Helen mused. And cursed Marina again, a silent but scathing, barbarous curse.

Then Dane replied to the string of questions, and Helen once again wished fervently that she could vanish in a puff of smoke. It was just too, too embarrassing.

'Oh, Helen's finished up her casual stint at the *Mercury*, so she's back to being a jillaroo again,' he said, making the comment—so casual in its wording—sound in Helen's ears like some form of condemnation.

It must have sounded so to Marina, too. 'And you celebrate that?' she asked, for the first time deigning to notice Helen's existence and making sure that Helen felt the scorn in her glance while ensuring that Dane didn't see it.

'Of course. A wake is something of a time-honoured journalistic tradition,' Helen replied, pleased to see how immediately Marina understood the intent of the remark. Helen and Dane were the journalists, united in tradition if nothing else, and Marina didn't like it.

'Well of course I'm all for tradition,' the brunette replied with a smile to Dane and a look at Helen that was anything but friendly. 'It's just that it seems ... well ... somewhat counterproductive to celebrate ... failure?'

'That's because you're not a journalist,' Dane remarked, and Helen could have kissed him for it. 'The end of a job, especially a casual one, isn't to be considered failure. Just the end of another career step; and by inference, of course, the beginning of yet another.'

'Well I should hardly call losing one's job and becoming a jillaroo much of a career,' Marina commented. But of course if you say so . . .'

'Oh for goodness' sake,' Helen burst in, unable to restrain her growing temper much longer. 'It isn't a career at all; it's nothing more than a purely temporary situation. Very temporary.'

'Ah, but at least it's something you enjoy,' Dane interjected. 'Most people can't say that even if they have got careers.'

Marina, Helen could tell, was far more interested in the concept of *temporary* than in any aspect of whether Helen was enjoying herself or not. But whatever the woman's next comment might have been, it was forestalled by the arrival of their waiter inquiring if they were ready for coffee and/or liqueurs.

And though Marina might have—and should have—taken this hint as an excuse to remove herself, she didn't. Nor did Helen expect she would have.

Maybe *I* should leave, Helen thought to herself. Certainly I'm not much more than a fifth wheel here, despite the fact it was supposed to be my celebration.

And for a moment, she thought seriously about doing just that. It would require no more than a pleaded headache, or tiredness. If nothing else, Dane would insist on driving her home, which would have the effect of breaking up this impossible little scenario.

But . . . why bother? It would only have the effect of creating a scene, however minor. And of embarrassing Dane, which she didn't want to do.

Helen was still pondering the situation when she realised that Marina was, rather belatedly, making the appropriate noises to indicate she knew she might be intruding, suggesting she really ought to leave them to their celebration.

To Helen's trained ear, it was inconceivably two-faced; Marina was obviously making the gesture in the hope and belief that Dane would invite her to stay. Which, Helen thought, he certainly would.

Only . . . he didn't! Unbelievably, he was agreeing with Marina, politely to be sure, but in such a way that she couldn't possibly pretend not to get his point. She didn't even try, but the look she shot at Helen was sulphurous in the extreme.

'Ah well, perhaps I'll see you next week?' she said in parting, the implication plain enough. She wanted to see Dane, but without Helen around to cramp her style. Not that I've even tried, Helen thought, unsure if she'd even want to, and equally sure that she did.

'Not next week, unless you're planning to be in Melbourne,' was the astonishing reply. Dane was going to Melbourne? And he hadn't so much as mentioned it, probably because of the assignation he was now so subtly arranging, Helen thought, and felt her heart shudder at the mental image of Dane and Marina snuggled down together in some classy Melbourne hotel.

And that's exactly what'll be happening, she thought, noticing that Marina neither confirmed nor denied any acceptance of the offer. Instead, the brunette merely smiled sweetly and made her farewells, giving the waiter a second chance to renew his offer of coffee.

Dane, suddenly effusive now that Marina had departed, insisted on coffee and the best available brandy. Helen would have been happier to have just gone home, despite the fact she could never think of Dane's house as home—not under these circumstances. Then she reconsidered; he had, after all, dismissed Marina when he didn't have to. So ... she would sit and make small talk if that's what he wished. She'd be doing so anyway; whether here or at the house couldn't make much difference.

'You didn't mention Melbourne before,' she began, and almost bit her tongue at the prying sound of what she'd said.

He grinned, and there was something wolfish, almost conspiratorial about the way he revealed white, even teeth, the way the laugh lines round his eyes twitched.

'Probably because I'd only just that moment thought it up,' he said. 'Although I have to go in any event, so next week's as good a time as any.'

'Yes, I can see that it would be easier all round, with me here to look after the animals,' Helen replied. 'And in another couple of weeks, well, with any luck I'll either be gone to a new job or right on the verge of going.'

'You don't have to make it sound as if I'm driving you away,' Dane said. 'This was your own idea, remember. Not mine. Far as I'm concerned, you can stay as long as you like.'

Helen smiled, hoping the smile covered the hurt inside at what she must reply. 'I . . . I don't somehow think it would work out too well if I did. It's fairly obvious that sooner or later I'd be just getting in the way.'

'That, my dear, is your opinion. And you're entitled to it no matter how ridiculous it is,' was the enigmatic reply. 'Especially if you're referring to our most recent interruption, although I can hardly expect you to think otherwise.'

'No,' Helen replied. 'I don't really think you should.'

Whereupon they both lapsed into silence, sipping at their coffee and brandy and gazing out at the slowly-revolving view. Helen knew that she was more retreating into herself than actually seeing what her eyes looked at, but she couldn't be at all certain whether Dane was lost in thoughts of his own or just determined not to continue a conversation that could only lead to dispute.

Even after they'd left the casino and begun the drive home, he seemed inordinately withdrawn, although she had to admit that her own silence didn't help much. The trip home seemed endless, with the big car speeding silently through the night with both driver and passenger locked into a conspiracy of silence.

It wasn't until they'd been greeted by a wriggling Labrador and had entered the kitchen that Dane finally spoke up, and his first comments set the tone of the conversation in a way Helen would have rather avoided . . . permanently.

'I'm really sorry about Marina's unexpected arrival tonight,' he said without preamble. 'Although frankly I can't understand why you insist upon being so damned jealous of her.'

'Well, that's good, because I'm not at all jealous of her,' Helen lied, hiding the lie in a savage smile. 'Well, perhaps that's not quite true. I certainly envy her that gorgeous hair.'

Infuriatingly, he only shrugged. 'You could get the same out of a bottle if you wanted it that badly,' Dane replied. 'Although I rather doubt if it would really suit you.'

'It wouldn't, and especially not out of a bottle,' Helen affirmed. 'Which Marina's isn't, as I'm sure you're quite well aware.' And she could have flinched at the pain that shot through her just at the thought of how he might ensure whether Marina was indeed a natural glossy brunette.

And Dane laughed, which was even more infuriating than his shrug. 'Is this the lady that just assured me a moment ago she wasn't jealous? She ought to envy you that ability to spread bulldust under any and all conditions,' he said. 'Although why you bother to try it on me, I'll never know. I'd have thought you'd have learned by now that it's a waste of time lying to me, because it never works.'

Oh, yes it does, Helen thought. And then, for just one truly frightening moment, wondered. What if it didn't? What if he really did know her thoughts, really did know her feelings? Then she shut her mind to that possibility, because it would make even one more night under his roof totally unbearable.

'I'd have thought you'd know by now that I seldom bother lying, and certainly never about important things,' she finally replied evasively.

'Oh, but of course. Why should I ever think of suggesting otherwise?' he remarked sarcastically, then paused as he shrugged off his dinner jacket and removed his tie. 'What about a night-cap?'

'I suppose so,' Helen replied without any genuine enthusiasm. Marina's interruption had put a distinct damper on her enthusiasm and Dane's silent drive home hadn't helped. She also thought she might have drunk too much wine, although at this particular moment she didn't feel as if she'd had a drop.

Dane poured their drinks, then excused herself for a few minutes and disappeared into his office. When he returned, two pieces of paper in hand, he handed them over with a slightly exaggerated flourish.

'What's this?' Helen asked, staring down at the two cheques in her hand.

'Housekeeping money for while I'm in Melbourne, and your wages, which I seem to have forgotten about until now.' Nothing in his tone allowed for the sizes of the two cheques, especially the one marked wages, and Helen looked back at him in astonishment.

'But ... but ...' She could go no further because it all made no sense at all. She hadn't earned nearly this amount as a jillaroo, much less as a houseguest, and she was already trying to find the words to say so when he interrupted.

'Well, dinner's in there too. You didn't really think I'd actually let you pay for it, did you? Hell, you've worked too hard for that money to fritter it away on food.'

'But I won the money to pay for dinner,' cried Helen, now quite confused by the situation. 'And besides, I *did* pay for it, and that's just as we agreed.'

'Just as you agreed. I was only having you on, really. I'd intended to take care of it all along. Especially since the uhm ... *tête-à-tête* we'd planned didn't excactly come off, eh? It would hardly be fair to expect you to be stuck with the bill for such a damnably interrupted fiasco.'

Helen reeled with astonishment at the apparent vehemence of his words. Surely he didn't feel as she did about Marina's gate-crash? He couldn't possibly, she thought; he was only being nice, trying to ease her all-too-obvious feelings.

'You make it sound like your girlfriend interrupted some great seduction scene,' she chuckled, and then chuckled again, quite unable to ignore the humour she saw in that particular scenario. Obviously Marina hadn't thought of it that way, or the brunette's attitude would have been even more unfriendly—if that were possible—than it had been.

'Actually, I was rather saving that for when we got home,' Dane said, stepping closer to her. Not aggressively, but there was something in his eyes that made Helen want to retreat and yet go to meet him, both at the same time.

Totally flustered, she flung out the first words that came to mind. 'Isn't it customary to stage seductions without expecting the girl involved to pick up the tab?' That much emerged unscathed, but some glint in his eye made her stammer over the rest of it: 'I mean, even . . . even paying her back later doesn't . . . doesn't make it workable, and especially not after your girlfriend has organised such a timely interruption.'

'Still on about her, are we?' But it wasn't a question. More like a warning; Dane's eyes had got hard, his mouth firm around the words.

He was close now, too close. Helen found herself retreating from the obvious anger, the stern look, the rigid muscles as he moved closer again, forcing her back and doing so deliberately.

'Running again, dear Helen? You seem to be doing a lot of that, lately, I think. That, or else throwing up Marina in my face at every possible opportunity. Even when you're denying you're jealous. I think maybe when I get back from Melbourne we might just have a little sort of straightening out session, see if you can't find something of the Helen I remember.'

'And just what's that supposed to mean?' Helen cried, using his speech to step around to one side, giving herself more room to manoeuvre.

'Fairly obvious, I should think. Either you've changed rather dramatically since I last saw you, which seems unlikely on the face of it. Or you've changed rather dramatically—and damned quickly—since your arrival here. Now that,' he grinned devilishly, 'is far more likely. I could even speculate on why, except that it would only make you angry, and probably frustrate me worse than I am already.'

'I think you're imagining things,' Helen replied, almost shouting at him in her desire to have this conversation stopped, and soon. It was far too close to the truth for comfort. Her mind raced, seeking something . . . anything . . . that she could say to diffuse the growing confrontation.

'Except for one thing. I do truly think you're *frustrated*,' she snapped. 'Which is why I wonder why you stand around arguing with me when your girlfriend is so obviously ready to cater to that particular need, among others.' Oh, it was bitchy. And she knew it. But she didn't care, not now.

'And I do truly think that you're just about ready to have your tidy little butt paddled,' Dane snapped in reply, one strong hand snaking out to capture her wrist. 'You're getting just a bit too big for your britches, *young* Helen, and it's about time you realised that if you act like a child you'll be treated as one.'

'Don't you dare!' Helen flailed out at him, but with a glass in her only free hand, her first reaction was not to spill the drink all over the floor, and her attempt at defensive manoeuvres was fruitless.

'Put the glass down.' His voice was grim, forbidding. His eyes now were like two chips of ice, while her own, Helen knew, would be enormous pools of grey velvet, startled and fearful.

'No! No, I won't. And if you don't let go, you'll be wearing this drink,' she cried.

She was remembering only too well how he'd paddled her out by the woodpile, and worse, what had followed that spanking. Were similar events to begin here, now, she knew she'd have no chance of resisting, wouldn't even want to try. And yet she'd have to, somehow.

'Only if you promise to abandon this insane jealousy

you keep insisting on exhibiting.' Still the grimness in the voice, but his eyes laughed. He was enjoying this, Helen thought.

'I am not jealous. And I never was. Why the hell should I be?' she retorted. 'It's nothing to me if you sleep with every brunette in Tasmania, just so long as you leave . . .'

'Just so long as I leave *you* alone? Yes, I rather thought so,' he interrupted, and now there was something else in the voice, something that cried out with pain, only Helen chose to interpret it as sarcasm.

'Right!' she cried, yanking free her wrist from a grip that suddenly slackened, making it easy for her to do.

It was a short-lived, transient freedom. Dane plucked the glass from her fingers even as he released her wrist, reached out to deposit it safely on the kitchen counter, and was once again totally in control of their confrontation before Helen could step free of his approach.

'You just seem bound and determined to push me right to the limits of endurance,' he said, voice in a soft, almost growling tone. 'But you never want to tell me why, which is surprising. We always used to be able to communicate rather well, I thought.'

'Maybe by your standards,' Helen replied, now backed against the wall, her entire body alive to the aura of his nearness and her entire mind alert to the need to defend herself, to keep him from luring her into a betrayal of her own safety.

'But not by yours? Oh, I don't think so,' he replied, and now his face loomed above her own, his eyes demanding her attention, his very presence authoritative, almost but not quite menacing.

'Although . . .' His voice seemed softer now, perhaps because Helen was drowning in his eyes, perhaps because he was deliberately infusing some seductive magic into both voice and glance. 'At least in the old days you'd have no trouble explaining why you feel it so important to leave. Now, apart from your obvious jealousy, you don't seem able to provide any reason at all.'

'That's ... that's ridiculous,' she stammered in reply. And shrank away from him as far as the wall behind would allow. 'I ... well ... surely you can't expect me to abandon my entire career just to be around here and handy whenever you need an animal-sitter.'

'Your ... career?' And somehow he injected just enough scorn into the word to get Helen's hackles up. How dare he be so deliberately condescending, just because she'd been out of work occasionally?

'Yes ... my career!' She spat out the words, anger building now to combat the fluttering of her heart, the sheer weakness his close physical presence so easily created. It was a weakness, she knew, that must never be allowed to dominate her reactions, lest she be forever lost to her own emotions and his ability to manipulate them.

And yet ... was he totally to blame? His offer of a place to live, a time to regroup, had undoubtedly been genuine and even unselfish. Was it his fault that she'd found herself falling in love? His fault that those feelings wouldn't and couldn't be returned?

'Oh, please don't misunderstand,' she said then, capitulating in the face of quite justifiable anger on his part even though he'd shown no real sign of that anger. 'I know you got me here with the best of intentions, but I can't stay indefinitely and you must realise that. It's ... well, it's time I moved on, got another job and started living my own life. I can't just hang about and sponge off you.'

'Sponge? Good lord, Helen, I certainly don't think you're sponging. You're paying your way and more, and surely you've no need to feel guilty in that respect.'

'It isn't a matter of feeling guilty. It's a matter of simple logic. I'm a journalist, not a jillaroo, not a cook, not a housekeeper. A journalist! And it's high time I went back to being a journalist, instead of hiding out from my responsibilities and evading them.'

Damn him, she thought, almost in tears at the frustration of having to be so evasive. But what else could she do? It would be the height of folly to admit that she couldn't stay because she had fallen in love with him—even *without* the involvement of the glamorous Marina Cole.

'I see.' But he didn't, Helen was sure. Although ... he did step back, did allow her at least a bit of breathing space, a chance to try and regain her composure.

'Well, I suppose I can't argue too much with that sort of logic,' Dane said. 'Provided, of course, that you're at least going to be sensible and stick around until you've *got* a job, not go hieing off to subsist on the dole somewhere else in the meantime. And don't deny that you're just stubborn enough to do it, either.'

Then he grinned, an unexpectedly warm and genuine grin, without the wolfish intensity he usually revealed. 'Besides,' he said. 'You haven't finished the kitchen remodelling project, and if you're not here I won't be able to go to Melbourne, will I?'

'That's blackmail, pure and simple,' Helen retorted, but she couldn't maintain her earlier anger. Of course it was blackmail, but she knew he wasn't being totally serious. If a job offer did arrive, he'd have no complaints whatsoever about having to make other arrangements to facilitate his Melbourne visit.

'Of course it's blackmail, but I expect that kitchen plan to be finished when I get back from Melbourne, or else I won't have a hope of getting the project completed by Christmas. And I want it done by Christmas.'

What's so important about Christmas, Helen wondered, but didn't ask. If he wanted her input into the plans, he could have it. Anything, so long as it reduced the tension and pressure of her current existence.

'I'm just about finished now,' she said. 'And certainly I can get it all together by the time you're done in Melbourne. I'd have done so sooner, but you never told me there was actually a starting date or anything.'

'There wasn't ... until now. But I've just decided it would be nice to have the extension done and finished for Christmas, so why not aim at that?'

'Why not indeed? If that's what you really want, that is. I suppose I could even get my plan drawn up within a day or two; I had it pretty well thought out at one point.'

'You can finish that up while I'm in Melbourne,' was the reply. 'Tomorrow, we'll take a holiday, maybe drive down to the Tasman Peninsula and play at being tourists for the day. I really feel I could use a day like that, and certainly you could, judging from how much you enjoyed your excursion with young Jones.'

'Well then I suggest an early night, or what's left of one,' Helen replied, half relieved and half sorry that their conversation had strayed on to much safer ground. Certainly this wasn't the finale she'd imagined for their evening out, but then she hadn't imagined the gate-crashing of Marina Cole would be possible, much less as effective as it had been in destroying the mood of the evening. On the other hand, she hadn't missed Dane's baiting comment about Geoff Jones, but she was damned and double-damned if she'd let herself be drawn into a discussion on that subject.

'An early night? You didn't need an early night before you went driving with young Jones,' Dane grinned, deliberately not letting her off the hook, determined to provoke some reaction from her.

'At our age, you can get by on very little sleep,' she replied, the taunt coming out even as she thought of it, even as she realised she was being drawn into his trap. Then, backpedalling quickly, she tried to talk herself out of the situation. 'But I think I'd have enjoyed that outing a great deal more if I'd had a decent night's sleep before it,' she continued, speaking quickly, ignoring the contradictions. 'I was half asleep most of the time, so I think I missed some of the best scenery.'

Dane shook his head as if in understanding sorrow at her feeble attempt. 'You mean you had too much grog with lunch at Oyster Cove,' he said. 'I could have warned you about that, and Jones damned well should have, although I suppose having you sleepy rather more suited his purpose.'

'I fail to see what that has to do with tomorrow,' Helen replied, knowing only too well what he was implying, but hoping she could talk her way out of it now, firmly and decisively.

'Considering I'm so much older than Geoff Jones, and you, I suppose not very much,' was the response, and she could see now that he was deliberately baiting her, and worse—enjoying himself immensely while he did so. Helen was tempted, but refrained.

'Just so long as you're as good a tour guide; that's what's most most important,' she replied. 'In fact, maybe I should do the driving . . .'

'The way you drive,' Dane interrupted, 'I'd need more than a good night's sleep to prepare me for such an ordeal.'

Then he laughed to show he wasn't totally serious, and turned away from her, stepping back to pick up his own glass from the kitchen table and hand Helen's over from the counter. 'But you're right, perhaps,' he said then, surprising her with his easy agreement. 'It's a fair drive if you want to see everything in just one day, so we'll need a fairly early start.'

He finished his drink in one gulp, then stepped forward to drop a light kiss on Helen's cheek before she could think to resist, muttering 'Good night, young Helen,' and exiting the room before she could do more than mutter a good night of her own.

She stood there for what seemed a very long time, conscious of the brief touch of his lips against her cheek, but even more conscious of the strange, up-and-down trend of their conversation. Was it deliberate, she wondered? A specific attempt to put her off balance and keep her there? And yet ... why? It just didn't make any sense.

She thought about it again later as she waited for sleep to claim her, but even when Dane knocked on her bedroom door at sunrise, she felt none the wiser. Only just as confused as ever.

It was a perfect day for such an excursion. The sky was clear and the brilliant blue that had come to symbolise Tasmania to Helen. In the distance, the hills picked up the blue tones, seemingly mist-covered, or bathed in swaddlings of pale smoke.

Dane, dressed comfortably in jeans and a light checked shirt, already had a light breakfast on the table when Helen emerged, and together they made short work of the meal and the farm chores that were required.

Once through Hobart and on to the Arthur Highway, heading almost due east through Midway Point, across the causeway to Sorell, Dane drove quickly but with his usual care, slowing only to point out what scenery he thought significant. The highway soon took them into fairly heavily timbered country, then abruptly dropped down through the Forestier Peninsula and to the narrow isthmus called Eaglehawk Neck.

This, according to the guidebook Dane had given Helen to help follow their travels, was where a military guard and savage dogs had been stationed to prevent the escape of convicts from the historic penal settlement at Port Arthur, further to the south.

Looking at the scene in brilliant daylight, with children playing on the sandy beaches that fronted both sides of the isthmus and their parents watching quietly from a variety of roadside parking areas, it was a feat of imagination to visualise what it must have been like during the mid-1800s, when more than twelve thousand convicts were imprisoned on the Tasman Peninsula under conditions shockingly harsh by any standard.

It was easier to relate to the scenic wonders, like the water-worn Tessellated Pavement, a unique geological feature just north of the narrow isthmus where nature had created a pavement in tidal rock formations as evenly and prettily as any human intervention could have managed.

Even easier was the frivolous 'Doo Town', where dozens of holiday shacks had followed a tradition of selecting names that incorporated the word 'Doo' in one fashion or another. Some of the names were fanciful, others painfully cliché-ridden, but all good for a giggle and somehow appropriate to Helen's mood.

The magnificent natural phenomena of the Blowhole, Tasman's Arch and the Devil's Kitchen, all strikingly beautiful if rather fearsome examples of the power of the sea that on this day slid quietly against cliffs it had once carved with an angry hand, were all worth the drive from Hobart all by themselves, in Helen's view. She found the natural sculptures both entrancing and delightful, and would have been happy to spend the day just exploring that one small area.

'Perhaps another time, because I have to share your feelings about it,' Dane said, 'but today is for having a more general look round.'

Which they did, driving back to Eaglehawk Neck, then turning west to drive along the top of the peninsula through scenic orchard and forest country, then on to a series of decreasing roads to the peninsula's remote northwest tip, where the ruins of a penal settlement and convict coal mines revealed little of their sordid past except to the imagination. Neither Helen nor Dane found the ruins especially impressive, except for the haunting, lonely, remoteness of the place, the feeling that so much and yet so little had really changed here since the days when Australian and British convicts of the worst type were punished by enforced labour in the mines.

Turning back, Dane seemed determined to turn Helen's interest to her surroundings, to the scenic aspects of the drive as they returned to Premaydena and then turned south to Nubeena and the tavern where he'd promised her the finest of seafood lunches.

The licenced Nubeena Restaurant specialised in using locally-caught fish and seafood, and Helen found herself facing difficult choices from the extensive menu. In the end, however, she took Dane's suggestion and opted for the local crayfish, and had to laugh when he produced a pair of nutcrackers from one pocket to help her crack the claws and legs.

By the time the meal ended, she felt as if she must be covered in bits of crayfish, which was never designed, she said, for dainty appetites. Dane only laughed, saying that he'd never noticed her appetite to be dainty at the best of times.

The best consolation was that several other diners seemed to envy her the facility of the nutcrackers, and certainly nobody else was bothering to be overly dainty either. It was, she thought, one of the best meals she'd ever enjoyed, even to the point of having no room left over for dessert.

'You can walk it off when we get to Port Arthur,' Dane told her as they left the restaurant for the thirteen-kilometre drive to Port Arthur, the most significant and historic of the peninsula's tourist attractions.

Historically, it was a fascinating place to spend an afternoon. But Helen found herself almost psychically aware of the looming, brooding air of despair that still hung over the ruins. It was only too easy to imagine the savage labours of the men who'd slaved to build their own prison surroundings and maintain themselves under conditions of stark severity.

'It seems so tragic that such a beautiful setting could have been wasted on such a purpose as a penitentiary,' she said at one point during their tour. 'Even now, the misery and harshness seem to overshadow the scenic attractiveness.'

Dane, not surprisingly, agreed. 'It's little consolation to know with hindsight that the guards didn't have it much easier than the prisoners,' he said.

Historically, this was true. Literature available was quite specific in detailing the hardships—such as floggings—that soldiers stationed at the penal settlement faced long after such punishments had been replaced with other methods of discipline for recalcitrant prisoners.

Dane, too, seemed affected by the dour atmosphere of the whole place, an atmosphere that even bus-loads of tourists and hordes of chattering, lively children couldn't quite dispel. When Helen flatly refused to take the ferry trip to the Isle of the Dead, where the attraction was little more than convict graves and convict-built headstones, he nodded understandingly.

'I've been here about three times, in weather ranging from a day as lovely as today to a blowing, howling winter southerly, and I still find the place amazingly depressing,' he said. 'I don't know whether it's some hereditary guilt feeling or what, but I find I can only take the place in small doses, which is why I left it 'til this afternoon; it does absolutely nothing for the kind of appetite I prefer when dining at Nubeena.'

Helen could only agree. The tourist literature described how Port Arthur had been struck by two major bush-fires after its abandonment as a penal settlement in 1877, and she found herself thinking it might have been better had the fires totally destroyed the settlement, rather than leaving reclaimable reminders of a history so fraught with pain and suffering.

And yet, historians would have totally disagreed, and maybe it was better for future generations to have some reminder of their history, however tragic.

Either way, Helen personally wasn't sorry when they drove north again on the way home, Dane driving slowly to ensure they would see whatever scenic attractions they might have missed on the outward journey, and as if by tacit agreement, discussing only the scenery, and not the historic monument behind them.

'It's good to get out and about again,' he said at one point. 'I think the thing I like best about Tasmania is the inevitable variety; almost every time you turn a corner there's something new to see, some aspect that's quite totally different than where you've just been.'

Coming as she had from a childhood on the wide, empty plains of western New South Wales, Helen couldn't help but agree with his feelings. The wide emptiness she remembered from her childhood also had a particular unique beauty, but variety of the type offered by Tasmania certainly hadn't been a part of it. In the western districts, the variety had been of a far more subtle type, the tracings of colour, the difference in textures of the rock and the light. Here, the very landscape provided a variety that changed with every passing kilometre; two sides of the same hill could appear to be in different climates, with quite distinctive forest growth and outlook.

'Yes, I'm not surprised it's such a popular tourist attraction,' she said, leaning back into the car's comfortable seat and feeling the relaxed atmosphere of the day sink into her like a sedative. 'You almost feel that you could spend years here and still never see everything there is to see.'

'And yet you're bound and determined to get away from it,' Dane replied, keeping his voice flat, almost totally without emphasis, and yet somehow the comment seemed to Helen to be an accusation of sorts.

'If I could get the right job here, I'd stay without a qualm,' she replied, knowing it was half a lie, knowing that it would be Dane himself, not just a job that could hold her in Tasmania without any questions at all. 'But I can't, so there's no logic in thinking about it. I'll just have to try and see what I can while I have the opportunity.'

Dane shrugged. 'If that's the case, maybe I should put off this Melbourne trip for a bit,' he said. 'I've been rather looking forward to showing you some of the best parts myself, but if you're so determined to move on, there mightn't be the time.'

'Oh, I think there's no great rush,' Helen replied without really thinking about what she was saying. 'On my track record, I don't expect anybody to rush in with hordes of job offers or anything like that.' Then she realised what she'd said, how she'd completely denied the urgency of her departure even while knowing that she must leave soon, that she couldn't possibly stay on with growing tension between herself and Dane, with Marina Cole always and increasingly present as an element of dissension between them.

And while she wished she hadn't been quite so casual in her comment, it was too late now. To retract would only make things worse. Thankfully, Dane hadn't appeared to notice her casual denial of the staunch principles she'd been advocating the evening before.

Most of the way home, he drove in silence, and Helen nearly fell asleep at one point, so relaxing had she found their day together. Once home, both declared that the luncheon was fully sufficient to last until morning, so they rushed through the chores and by the time Dane had returned from a long walk with Molly, Helen was sound asleep.

Dane spent the next two days editing his manuscript and preparing for his Melbourne visit, and Helen did her best to stay out of his way. Most of her time she spent with either dog or donkey, revelling in the fine spring weather, the fresh air and the relative solitude of the farm.

By the time he returned from Melbourne, she reasoned, there would surely be word of some kind from the jobs she'd applied for, and he'd also promised

to check around some of his contacts in the Victorian
capital to see what opportunities he could find for her.

And, if nothing else, there had been two more
possibles in that weekend's paper, neither of them jobs
she would normally have considered, but now almost
any journalist's job must be looked at seriously. The
longer she stayed with Dane, the less she truly wanted
to leave and the more she became positive that she must
. . . and soon.

He, himself, would be leaving later today, and as he
emerged from his office, tidily dressed for the journey,
he paused to pick up the latest two application letters
and tuck them into his suit coat pocket.

'I'll drop them in the mail when I get to Melbourne,'
he said. 'And now we'd best be off or I'll miss my
plane.'

They said little on the way to the airport, apart from
the expected domestic conversation, but when he'd
parked the car, Dane turned to Helen with an unusually
serious expression on his face.

'Are you going to miss me?' he asked. 'I mean, really
miss me?'

'I . . . well . . . of course,' Helen replied, even as his
lips moved to forestall anything else she might have
said. Their touch was so gentle, so . . . right, that she
could only meet them with all the feeling inside her,
without trying to hide any of the love she felt. Instinct
governed reason for the minute it took him to trap her
with that unexpected kiss.

'That's good, because I'm going to miss you. More
than I think you realise,' he said softly. 'But now isn't
the time to talk about it. Don't come to see me off,
love. Just be here to pick me up when I return, because
there's a lot I want to say to you.'

And he was out of the car, striding away without
looking back, before Helen could find the words in her
suddenly numbed mind to even think of a reply.

CHAPTER EIGHT

HELEN watched, as if in a dream, as Dane's powerful figure weaved through the parking lot, across the street and into the domestic terminal building.

Had this really happened? Had he truly kissed her in just *that* way . . . called her 'love' in just that way . . . promised . . .?

She shook her head, blonde hair flying across her suddenly misty eyes. No, she thought. It had meant nothing. Couldn't mean anything. He hadn't even looked back.

Still, the imagery haunted her mind throughout the long drive back to the farm, and throughout the day's endless evening and longer, sleepless night, she found her mind constantly returning to re-run the scene . . . over and over and over. It was almost a form of torture; she was torn between the logic that said his actions and words had to mean *something*, and the logic that said they didn't have to at all.

He didn't telephone. Helen really hadn't expected him to, and if he had, it would only have added to her confusion. As, indeed, it did when he 'phoned the next night, waking her from the first decent sleep she'd had since his departure.

'I woke you up, didn't I?' The familiar chuckle in the voice, the knowing, familiar tones for some reason got her back up just enough to reply, 'No, I was out on the verandah watching the stars.'

He only chuckled again, the sound amplified by the indistinct telephone line. 'Why do you try to fib all the time, dear Helen? You really ought to know better by now; it just doesn't work with me.'

'All right. I was asleep and you woke me up.

Does that satisfy you?'

'I thought you were out on the porch, watching the stars? And thinking of me, I hope.' There was just that hint of pure, sadistic mockery in his voice, just enough to provoke her.

'Well you can't have it both ways,' she snapped. 'So just make whatever choice suits you; it doesn't matter much anyway.'

'Now you're getting shirty,' he said. 'Of course it matters. So I'll choose ... outside thinking of me. How's that?'

'Whatever you say,' Helen sighed, suddenly only too aware of the distance between them. If she had been thinking of him, it would only have been to wish he was there with her, not talking on a telephone all the way across Bass Strait and most of Tasmania to boot. And the lilt in his voice as he tormented her now didn't improve anything.

'My, but that sounds promising,' he muttered, voice think with unconcealed sarcasm. 'I thought you said you'd miss me.'

Helen had to laugh. 'You've only been gone a day and a half,' she said, unwilling to admit just how much she did miss him. 'If you expect me to miss you that much already, what would I be like by the end of the week?'

'Probably about as lonely as I am for you already,' was the unexpected, almost unbelievable reply. 'I do miss you, Helen, and it isn't going to get any easier by the end of this week or any other.'

'I ... well ...' She was flabbergasted, unable to believe her ears. Was he drinking? Drunk, even? No, not from the voice. And certainly not from her knowledge of his usually careful habits.

Dane didn't give her any more chance to think about her reply. 'And I'm halfway now to starting that discussion I said would have to wait 'till I get back,' he said. 'And it will have to wait; just so long as you do.

So good night, my love. Sleep tight and don't forget to meet me Tuesday.'

And he was gone. As abruptly as he'd left her at the airport, and with yet another alluring, infuriatingly unclear message. Helen, in her soul, desperately wanted to believe what his comments on both occasions implied.

She sat, holding the buzzing receiver, for seconds after Dane's voice had disappeared, her mind awhirl with the disbelief and the belief, the wonder of it all. For the rest of that week and into the weekend, she hovered near the telephone every evening, *willing* him to 'phone again, begging him in a rush of sudden, heart-full pleading.

And although her cautious nature forced her to rationally suspect she might be leading herself up the proverbial garden path, her heart slowly gained the edge, her need of Dane and his love took a firm foothold.

But he didn't 'phone. Not even on Friday evening. Not even after she'd blithely declined an invitation from Geoff Jones—who interested her not at all, but could at least have helped stave off her growing loneliness.

By Saturday, Helen would have telephoned Dane, except that she hadn't the faintest idea where to find him. Was he staying with friends? In an hotel? For the life of her she couldn't even remember if he'd mentioned anything.

The fact that the Saturday morning newspapers suddenly gave her worries of a totally different nature didn't help either. She had bought the weekend papers through habit, and was scanning the job advertisements with only cursory interest when one notice caught her eye.

It was certainly one of the jobs she'd first applied for—and it was being re-advertised! Now this was a mystery indeed, she thought, chewing pensively at a cooling piece of toast. Because this was definitely one job for which she'd been ideally qualified.

'And they didn't even answer my letter!' she cried suddenly as awareness struck her. That, she thought, added to the mystery. Usually a re-advertisement could be taken to mean that no one who'd applied the first time round was reasonably qualified, and yet when she consulted her file of clippings, comparing the original advertisement against the second one, it merely served to confirm that she had been, if anything, a touch *over*-qualified.

The situation nagged at her throughout the morning, and by eleven o'clock curiosity won. It was a long-shot to expect to find the editor in his office, and she didn't, but directory assistance took only moments to provide her with a home number and she dialled it immediately.

As she knew the man only by reputation, she was mildly surprised to find that he appeared to know her—or at least of her work—also. But the biggest surprise was yet to come.

'My dear Miss Fredericks,' he said in answer to her question. 'If I had received your letter, you can be sure that I would have replied, and that if you'd been available I wouldn't be in the position of re-advertising the position. No question at all. Good people, at the moment, are practically impossible to come by, and *you* ... well ...' Then, to make the situation even more mysterious, he went on to explain that a compatriot of his was also faced with re-advertising a position—and this *too* was one for which Helen had applied!

'I ... look, do you mind if I get back to you on this?' she found herself asking. And nearly kicked herself for not just grabbing the vacancy. It was certainly the best of all those she'd enquired about, and yet ... no, she must first try to ascertain how not only one letter of application, but two, had so mysteriously gone missing. Australia Post wasn't the most reliable postal service in the world, but ...? There were too many loose ends here.

'My dear, the job's yours if you want it until ... noon Monday? And if you need a bit more time, don't hesitate to call,' said the editor. 'In fact, where can I contact you, just so we don't miss each other through some other extraordinary bit of confusion?'

'Look, I'm ... sort of staying with a friend,' Helen found herself replying. 'And I'm not just sure where I'll be by Monday. But don't worry, I'll get back to you. It's just that ... well ... there are one or two things I must square away first.'

Not least of which, she thought, was whether she *really* wanted to work in Adelaide, despite having always thought it was a beautiful city. In fairness, she didn't want to leave Tasmania, especially now, in view of Dane's cryptic comments over the phone and on his departure.

After her talk with the editor, Helen sat back and reviewed all of Dane's comments in her mind. Disregarding her own feelings, her hopes and dreams, it was all too possible that all he wanted to do was assure her of a place to stay as long as she needed it. Not only possible, but highly likely, she finally decided, especially when she allowed her logical mind to put Marina Cole into the picture.

After his excellent marriage to Vivian, and with a sophisticated, attractive social partner already on tap, why indeed should he even consider getting involved with somebody he'd always thought of and treated almost as a child?

Helen thought then of his caresses, and put them down to sheer proximity. 'I'd be a damned fool to think otherwise,' she muttered. 'And worse than a fool if I turned down a perfectly good job on the strength of a kiss or two.'

She had probably, in fact, been somewhat of a fool to have come to Tasmania at his request in the first place. She'd known of her feelings for him, should have realised and predicted exactly what had happened.

'Yes, I should have, so I've only myself to blame,' she told Joshua as she ran the chocolate-coloured donkey through his paces that evening. 'Of course if I hadn't come, you'd still be wild and woolly and free-spirited, so I guess there's something good come out of it all, even if you don't agree.'

The donkey snuffled at her fingers, then brayed hoarsely as if in agreement. 'If only I could take you with me, I would,' Helen sighed. 'but I can't, and that's all there is to it. I've barely got enough funds to get myself to the mainland, let alone take you as well.'

She had just finished Joshua's workout and her chores and was returning to the house when she heard the faint tingling of the telephone. It was Dane! It had to be, she thought, running for the back door with both arms filled with a rickety basket of eggs she'd forgotten to collect that morning.

Three of them were sacrificed in her desperate bid to get the door open, and it was all in vain, because the telephone stopped ringing just as her fingers grasped the receiver.

'Damn,' she cried, more angry than she needed to be about having dropped the eggs and even more angry at the telephone's antics. She cleaned up the mess, then brewed some coffee and sat down to wait. If it had been Dane, he'd surely ring again, realising where she'd have been at this time of evening, Helen thought. And if it was anyone else, well, she could only wait and see.

But whoever it was, they didn't ring back, and she ate a pensive, lonely meal and spent an even lonelier evening, waiting for Dane to ring, hoping desperately he'd ring, yet somehow knowing that he wouldn't, somehow knowing that despite her dreams and her love for him, she would be telephoning Adelaide first thing Monday and accepting the job she'd been offered.

The question of who had rung was answered when the 'phone jangled Helen out of bed first thing Sunday morning. It was an old friend of Dane's, a man she'd

never met but had heard of, and he first apologised for
calling so early, then mentioned having telephoned the
evening before.

'What I need is an address, and Dane's the only
person I'm sure will have it,' he said. Helen, loath to
rummage through Dane's office on any pretext, finally
allowed herself to be persuaded to 'at least have a quick
look'. And she was immediately, madly, astonishingly
glad she had!

Finding the directory and providing the caller with
the address was incidental, completely so. What was
important was her finding in the same drawer all the
application letters he'd promised to mail weeks ago.
And worse, the two she'd thought he'd taken with him
on the day of his departure for Melbourne!

That, she decided, was quite enough to eliminate any
thought of the first lot being just a mistake, something
he'd intended to mail and forgotten.

She thought back, remembering how on the eve of his
departure for Melbourne he'd dashed back into the
house at the last minute, claiming to have just forgotten
something. Forgotten? He'd damned well deliberately
arranged it, not simply forgotten. But why? What
possible purpose could be served by him delaying any
chance she might have of finding a job? Frustration
combined with sheer, impotent rage at the effrontery of
such a thing, but it did little to offer an explanation.
For Dane, of all people, to deliberately deceive her in
such a fashion ... it was beyond all imagination. It
simply made no sense.

Then there was a knock at the door and Molly's
barking to announce the visitor, and when Helen
answered to find Marina Cole there, she had the unholy
feeling that she mightn't have to wait long for her
explanation.

But Marina's first comment brought only more
confusion, although not for long.

'You're not expecting me,' the tall brunette began,

eyes suddenly evasive, brimming with ... could it be guilt? Or just pure satisfaction, Helen wondered.

'I wasn't, no. Should I be?' Helen stepped aside to usher Marina into the kitchen, suddenly all too aware of her lick-and-promise housekeeping and the fact she hadn't yet bothered to wash up the breakfast dishes.

'Well ... I would have thought so. But then, perhaps Dane thought we should discuss this ... oh, you know woman-to-woman. That sort of thing. Although I did rather expect he'd have telephoned.'

Marina seemed slightly vague, but Helen felt sure it was a deliberate ploy, a bid to keep herself off balance. But why?

Whatever, she wasn't in any mood to co-operate. 'I'm sorry, but I simply don't understand what you're getting at,' she replied firmly. 'And well, I'm rather busy, so ...'

'You haven't arranged a job yet?' Marina asked then, the question so startlingly, provocatively unexpected Helen couldn't even reply for gasping. 'Oh, I certainly hope not. Dane was quite worried about it while we were together in Melbourne, you know.' And the look of concern was Marina *trying* to look concerned. Helen was convinced the woman didn't have a whit of genuine concern anywhere in her elegant body.

'I ... I certainly can't see why it should concern him,' she replied, damned if she'd snatch at the bait by asking what he and Marina had been doing together in Melbourne. The sultry brunette, Helen thought, would probably delight in nothing more than giving her chapter and verse.

Nor was she going to mention the evidence of Dane's perfidy; that would have been opening herself up to far too much pain and hurt, in view of this sudden revelation.

'Oh, but of course it does.' Marina's emphasis did little to ease Helen's growing tension. Where was this conversation leading, she wondered. And wasn't looking forward to finding out. But if Marina noticed her close-hidden concern, she gave no sign, and continued as if Helen should be equally excited by what she was saying.

'It's most important, because of the excellent job you've been doing here,' the brunette continued. 'I mean . . . with the animals and everything. And especially now!'

Helen hardly knew what to say. 'Are you deliberately being obtuse? Or is this something you'd really prefer me to hear from him personally?' she asked, herself being almost deliberately rude, but not really caring.

What *had* Marina and Dane been doing together in Melbourne? And more important, why should it concern her job or the lack of it?

Marina, unfortunately, didn't appear at all concerned by Helen's lack of cordiality. She continued speaking as if what she had to say was simply the most important thing in the universe. Which, Helen decided spitefully, it probably was . . . to Marina.

'Well of course it might have been better if Dane were to have told you,' the brunette said. 'But then, as I said, woman-to-woman . . . anyway, it's because of the trip he's—we're—planning. Of course that will require somebody to mind the farm in his absence.'

'Ah.' It was about all Helen could say, certainly all she wanted to say. So Dane was planning a trip, obviously not alone, and he wanted her to baby-sit the farm. Hardly a difficult subject for him to raise himself, apart from the direct slap in the face created by the fact he was taking Marina along and not Helen herself.

'A honeymoon?' The question wasn't meant to be asked aloud, so it emerged as a sort of ghastly whisper, wrung from Helen's strangled heart.

Marina simpered. It was a gesture Helen had thought no longer existed, but that was what Marina did. She simpered. 'Well it's perhaps a bit premature to call it exactly that,' the brunette smirked. 'But, well—you know . . .'

'Yes, I suppose I do,' Helen replied, gritting out the words and fighting with a stomach now roiling with emotion. But she wouldn't . . . couldn't let this horrible woman see the effect the message was having on her.

Marina didn't even seem to notice. She continued speaking with callous indifference to Helen's feelings. 'Of course, I realise that you might, when you got here, have entertained some such notion yourself,' the woman was saying. 'Although of course I'm sure that by now you realise what a mistake that might have been.'

'Oh, yes,' Helen agreed, restraining the urge to strike out both verbally and physically. It was all she could do to keep herself from grabbing up this voluptuous bitch and throwing her bodily out the door.

'Of course. I told Dane you'd understand,' Marina continued. 'And I could hardly blame you for having such feelings; he is *such* a catch, isn't he? But of course you're far too young for him, and not . . . quite the right type. I mean, a best-selling author should have the required degree of sophistication around him.'

Helen didn't reply. What could she say, after all?

But Marina wasn't finished yet. Not by a long shot. 'In fact, I wouldn't be surprised if once he's been away from *this* place for a while, he mightn't bother to come back. It really isn't much of a farm, after all. And as for the house . . . well . . .'

'He was planning to have the kitchen re-done.' Why had she said that, Helen wondered, clamping her jaw shut before she revealed that it was she who'd done the re-designing.

Marina looked around, disdainfully. 'Well I can certainly see why he might,' she sniffed. 'Although of course it won't matter now, except perhaps to the hired help.'

Like me, Helen thought, once again biting back that fierce resentment.

'And to think that his wife actually put up with such inconvenience,' Marina was saying, now seemingly oblivious to Helen as she cast a disapproving eye further. 'The entire house is something of a hovel, if you ask my opinion, but then perhaps his wife . . .'

'He loved his wife very much, and she felt the same about him,' Helen interrupted, astonished at her defence of Dane, then as quickly justifying the words by her own feelings for Vivian.

'Oh, but I'm sure he . . . they did,' Marina replied. 'And of course, perhaps then it was all they could afford, but now . . .'

Helen was sickened by the cold, mercenary attitude, although she was equally sickened just at the moment by Dane's betrayal of her, by his clearly and cleverly-planned deception.

How he had changed—must have changed—in the time since she'd last seen him. Could his success as an author have so altered him? It didn't seem possible, and yet this woman, her attitude, her words, and his blatant deception told a different story.

And to have the outright audacity to send this . . . this bitch to arrange the fruits of that deception. Well, he'd find out about that in good time. Not, of course, that he'd find out from Marina. Helen wouldn't give the woman the satisfaction of knowing she'd driven off a potential rival, even if considering herself such was— as clearly proven—the height of self-deception. No, she would agree with Marina, let her say whatever suited her. But she wouldn't be here on Tuesday to meet Dane at the airport. Marina could do that, so as to share with him the realisation that the deception hadn't worked after all.

As anger formed an icy block inside her, Helen found herself more and more tempted to personally throttle her unwelcome visitor, but of course she couldn't do that. So instead she determined to see just how much more information she could get from Marina.

'May I ask just how long this little expedition is planned to be?' she said. 'The idea obviously is that I'm to care for the farm while you're away, so it would be nice if I had some idea of how long that will be.'

Marina shrugged. 'Oh, perhaps six months. Maybe longer, as I really can't imagine Dane actually coming back here to live, you understand.'

What Helen understood was that Marina certainly wouldn't come to live at the farm; Dane's feelings on the subject were clearly not paramount.

'I suppose that this plan to have me stay on as farm manager or whatever has something to do with the problems I've had recently in finding a new job?' Helen asked, unwilling to come right out with her evidence of Dane's deceit, but determined now to see if she could tie Marina into the conspiracy.

'Well, he did say something about it, but I'm not personally *au fait* with the exact situation,' Marina smirked. 'And really it doesn't matter, does it? I mean, you're quite happy here with your animals, and of course I'm sure the salary will more than compensate for any losses.'

Not in the long term, Helen thought. She'd already been out of regular work too long, from a purely positive career viewpoint. And Dane would have known that, too, yet he obviously didn't care. And he *should* care, damn him! He should!

She was beginning to think the entire situation of her being in Tasmania was part of the plot, and yet ... Marina hadn't known she was coming. That much, from memory, was certain.

'Yes,' Helen finally replied. 'Yes, I'm sure it will. And of course I get my keep thrown in as well, which is worth looking at. What I can't quite figure out is your involvement in this. I mean, Dane surely could have arranged to tell me himself; he gets back early on Tuesday.'

Marina was evasive, both in gesture and the drawn-out 'We-e-e-ll' she shrugged at Helen.

'But then I suppose you really wanted to be sure I understood that my tenure would have to ... end abruptly? On your return, that is.'

'Something like that. Although of course it will depend on whether we return to the farm or move into something more appropriate in the city. But really, I'd think it best all round if you were to consider yourself redundant about that time.'

Helen grinned. Not outside, where Marina could see it, but inside ... just to herself. 'Myself, I think it would be just about as logical to just leave now. After all, there isn't much logic to my staying in what I already know is a dead-end situation.' Then she paused momentarily before adding. 'Or would it be just too much to expect ... you looking after the place for the next day or two?'

'Quite impossible. Animals, I'm afraid, are not my line.' Marina paused, then, apparently considering the problem deeply. 'But of course I can see your position,' she finally added, 'and really I think I'd almost have to agree. Purely from a woman's point of view, of course. One really must look ahead to get ahead, and perhaps it's just a bit unfair of Dane to expect you to stay on ... under the circumstances. I'm sure that's why he wanted me to try and break the news to you gently.'

About as gentle as a sledge-hammer, Helen thought. But said, 'Yes, well I appreciate it, Miss Cole. I really do.'

Five minutes later, Helen was alone, sitting over a hastily-brewed cup of coffee and turning the whole conversation over and over in her mind.

It didn't make sense. Even trying to put herself in Marina's shoes, it didn't add up. Marina should have leaped at the bait, should have gone out of her way to ensure that Helen would leave as soon as possible. Sooner!

'Unless she's even more vindictive than I think,'

Helen muttered to herself. 'Maybe she just wants to be able to rub salt in the wounds.'

If nothing else, she now had a rationale to explain Dane's deliberate interference in her job-hunting, but that was small consolation. If any. She drank half the coffee, then stared the rest into frigid bitterness as she pondered his betrayal.

The bastard! The utter bastard. How could he possibly betray a friendship like that? Never mind her own romantic feelings ... she could live with the fact that they hadn't been returned. But to have so blatantly interfered with her career, with her future—that was unbelievable and totally unforgivable.

'Well, if nothing else, Marina will get her wish,' Helen said aloud, feeling the raggedness of anger in her voice. 'I don't give a damn who looks after this place while they're gone, but it won't be me. That, is for certain!'

She was less certain later in the day when she was out working with the animals, comfortable in the warmth of the sunshine and enjoying Joshua's antics despite the cloud of gloom that seemed to saturate her every pore. She had loved it here, she thought, and just for an instant considered staying on, despite the impossibility of it.

Then logic took over, combining with her bitterness and anguish. By midnight she was almost totally packed, and first thing next morning she was on the 'phone to Adelaide, accepting the job.

'I'll be flying in first thing tomorrow, with luck,' she told her new editor. 'So I can start Wednesday, if you like ... or leave it until first thing next week. Whichever suits.'

'Have you organised your flight yet?'

'No, but I'd like to get away as early as possible,' Helen replied. 'And certainly no later than noon. In fact, first thing in the morning or just before noon would be best.'

That way she could be sure of not meeting Dane in the airport at either end of the journey. Her own sense of responsibility to the animals in her care made it impossible for her to leave before the next morning; she wouldn't let the stock suffer by her own temper no matter how severe the motive. But she would definitely be gone before Dane arrived at the Hobart airport. She could easily enough leave a message for him with his airline, along with the keys to the vehicle she'd leave in the airport parking lot.

It took a few minutes more to arrange the flight itself, having the editor's permission to charge the costs directly to his newspaper, and the timing was perfect, from Helen's viewpoint.

She would actually be in the air, passing Dane's aircraft, *en route* to Melbourne, then be on her way to Adelaide about the time he'd be getting her message at the airline's Hobart office.

It would be, she decided, a very, very short message.

But the letter she must leave at home for him was longer, more complicated. And much, much more difficult to compose. Helen spent most of the day writing it, over and over and over. Each time different, each time less satisfactory than the one before.

It was impossible, she found, to put in writing her true feelings, either as they had been before his betrayal or even now, now that she could tell herself she was better off without any further involvement with a man who'd do such a thing. Even more impossible to mention Marina's visit, or even that she now knew what Dane had done with her job applications.

He'd find out anyway; she must relate the circumstances under which she'd invaded the privacy of his office and desk. Whatever else, she wouldn't have him thinking she was a sneak.

And in the end, her letter became the essence of simplicity. She told him of the 'phone call from the address seeker, and that she'd found a job at last, one that she had to grab immediately. 'So I left this morning, unfortunately before your arrival,' she wrote. Not telling him which job, or where. 'The animals have all been fed and watered and Molly, too. I'm sorry to be going in such a rush, but there was no other way. Thank you for your hospitality, and your help. I'll write as soon as I'm settled.'

She wouldn't write, Helen knew. Or at least not for a very long time. There just wasn't anything to say ... not any more.

Dane would know, of course, that she *knew* how he'd deliberately sabotaged her job-hunting. He'd know if for no other reason than because she was taking the un-mailed letters with her. What he wouldn't know—and must never know, never be allowed to know—was how much she'd allowed herself to be hurt, how vulnerable she'd become.

There was nothing in the letter to suggest it, and nothing she'd said to Marina would tell him. She'd found a job and she'd taken it. End of story. He might not appreciate being left to find a new farm manager, but he could hardly blame Helen for that, not after the underhanded methods he'd used to keep her there.

And at least this way she could escape without a personal confrontation, however much she thought—and immediately discarded those thoughts—that she'd love to throw the whole thing up in his face, just to watch him squirm. She'd love to do it, and indeed would love to be *able* to do it. But she never could, and never would, so she put those thoughts aside as swiftly as they arose.

By nine that evening, she was packed, organised and ready to leave as soon as the animals had been cared for next morning. And she was exhausted, as much by the strain of writing her departure letter as by the overall mental anguish of the whole, sordid mess.

She fairly fell into bed, consoling herself with the thought that in twelve hours she'd be on the way out of this predicament, heart-broken perhaps, but at least with the remnants of her pride intact.

There was time on her way to the airport to sort out final details of banking and the like, and she'd already prepared an envelope to be left for Dane with his airline. Her clothes for the morrow were laid out and ready; she need only do her chores, get showered and changed, and be gone.

Now all that remained was to sleep, and that she found most difficult of all. Her stomach was rolling, her head ached and she felt as if someone had been beating on her with a large, heavy stick. Nerves? Helen hoped it was only nerves. The last thing she needed now was a dose of the influenza that seemed to be going round.

She tossed and turned, got up and made a cup of warm milk, returned to bed no more able to sleep than before, and was sitting up, reading without taking in a single word, when the telephone rang.

She didn't answer at first, though she knew she must, eventually. And she knew, also, who'd be on the other end of the line. It was the final, crowning touch to an already horrid day, but she had no real choice—except in making the instant decision of what she'd say and what she wouldn't.

So she answered the 'phone on the sixth ring, and wasn't even remotely surprised when Dane's voice said, 'I woke you up, didn't I?'

CHAPTER NINE

'YES,' Helen said. It was easier than any explanation of why, otherwise, she'd have let the 'phone ring so long.

'Sorry,' he said, although he didn't sound it. 'But I thought I'd better confirm my arrival time tomorrow. It's just as we'd planned.'

'All right,' Helen said, keeping her voice carefully neutral. She couldn't, however, still the thundering of her heart. She might be angry with this man, might even hate him just a little, but damn it, she still loved him, too.

'You don't sound right,' he said. And she damned him for his perceptiveness before replying.

'I'm just ... well ... tired. You did wake me, after all.'

'You sound more than just tired to me. Is everything all right?'

'Of course it is,' she lied, forcing just enough defensiveness into her voice to give the impression of mild indignity.

'You're not upset because I've hardly 'phoned, or anything like that?' And his voice showed he didn't really believe her. He was, she decided, far, far too perceptive. She'd have to try and cut this conversation short, if he'd let her. Only knowing Dane, he'd pick just this time for a long talk, and to hell with the cost.

'I can't imagine why that should upset me,' she replied in a calm voice. 'You've only been away a few days, after all, and I'm quite capable of looking after myself. I've been doing it for years.'

'Yes, you're a big girl now, aren't you?' he chuckled. 'I keep forgetting that.'

Helen said nothing. What was there to say? But she

should have said something, and even as she intuitively realised that, she also realised it was too late.

'There *is* something wrong.' And now he was certain.

Damn him! Helen could just imagine him sitting there, every sense totally alert. He'd always been able to read her like a book, and now she must do something to invalidate his ability. And fast!

'You're imagining things,' she laughed, forcing it, but yet making the laughter sound genuine, effortless. Then a quick verbal shuffle, 'I think you must have been over-working. Was your trip the success you hoped . . . or have you just been carousing for a week?'

'Stop trying to change the subject.' His voice now grim, almost implacable. 'Now seriously . . . what's wrong? You haven't had prowlers or anything like that? Or . . .'

'I haven't had anything,' Helen replied stoically. 'I'm just tired and I'd really like to get back to sleep. Can't the inquisition wait until tomorrow?'

'It can not. Not if there's something wrong that I ought to know about now.'

'But there isn't. I've already told you that fifteen times,' she cried. 'Don't you listen? Can't you hear?'

'And I've told *you* a million times not to exaggerate,' he snorted. 'Why do you always insist on lying to me; you know it doesn't work? Now let's try it again—what's wrong?'

This is ridiculous, Helen thought. It doesn't matter what I say, he isn't going to believe it. But then . . . what does it matter? Now.

'If you must know . . . I'm pregnant,' she snapped. 'There—does that satisfy you?'

For an instant, the merest flickering of an instant, Helen thought she heard him gasp. But when he spoke, she knew she must have been mistaken. 'Is that all?' he said. 'Anybody I know?' Showing he didn't believe her and wasn't going to let go that easily either. Unless . . .

'Yes!' she cried. And hung up the 'phone, only to sit

there, trembling, until it rang again a few moments later. For a few seconds, she thought of just letting it ring, but common sense took hold. Let's get it over with, she thought.

'Were you serious?' And now his voice held something more than caustic sarcasm. Now he actually sounded worried. Not that he would be.

'No, I wasn't serious. It's just that if you insist on stupid questions, you'll get stupid answers,' she sighed. 'Now please, can we postpone this stupid discussion until later. I'd really like to get some sleep and you're spending a lot of money on this for no return at all.'

'You let me worry about money,' he growled. 'But ... all right. And if I find out when I get there tomorrow that you've been lying to me ... well heaven help you, young Helen.'

'I'm sure it will. Good night,' she said, and hung up almost in the middle of his response.

Five minutes later she was asleep, her final thoughts that at least the discussion appeared to have resolved her problem of insomnia; her other problems would sort themselves out in time.

The next day dawned with a cloudless sky and the promise of excellent weather ... at least in Hobart. But it was, Helen thought, a good omen. And for once she was right. The day went like clockwork, exactly as she'd planned, and there was even the unexpected pleasure of being met at the Adelaide airport by her new boss.

He was a large, solid, greying man in his late forties, a man to whom Helen took an instant liking. There was every indication he'd be a considerate employer, and he proved it immediately after greeting her when she stepped into the terminal.

'One of my girls is getting married on Saturday,' he said, 'and since you'll be taking over her work until she's back from her honeymoon, we thought you might be interested in taking over her flat, as well. Save you a lot of fuss and bother looking round for one.'

'Well I'll certainly have a look at it,' Helen replied. 'And probably take it, presuming the price is right, because there are few things I hate worse than flat hunting.'

Two hours later, it was settled. Judy, the girl being married, was to go home for the final few days of her single life, leaving Helen in possession of the flat and thus more than ready to begin work the very next day.

And the work, much to her delight, was rather different than she'd expected. On the basis of the advertisement, Helen had been indeed slightly over-qualified, but having seen her credentials, the editor had rearranged his staffing situation to put her into a variety of tasks she'd relatively little experience at, and Helen found the challenge both stimulating and engrossing.

Not so much that she could totally keep her mind from straying back to Tasmania, especially in the relative, city-noisy quiet of early morning. But enough to at least help her get through the days one at a time, gradually reconciling her loneliness and coming to terms with it.

But it was difficult. There were too many things, too many newsroom habits and journalistic comments and clichés that reminded her of Dane as she'd first known him, when he was honourable and decent and so very good to her. And too many nights when she'd lie sleepless, wondering if he knew where she'd gone, if he even cared.

A fortnight passed, and the worst of the pain with it. Until one lunch-time when she entered her favourite pub to hear her name called in a voice that seemed familiar.

'Geoff Jones! But ... what are you doing in Adelaide?' Helen wasn't sure at first if she ought to be pleasantly or unpleasantly surprised by the unexpected coincidence of meeting Geoff, but quickly decided. He was friendly, charming—and harmless. Good company without complications.

'Oh, I've been here a couple of weeks now. Came over on a special marketing thing; I'll be here another month or more. But what about you? Last I heard you were Dane's favourite jillaroo.'

'Oh no. I've been working here for the last fortnight,' she said. And a moment later determined that they'd arrived the same day on different aircraft.

'Quite a surprise, I must say. I thought you were pretty firmly entrenched,' Geoff remarked after going off to buy each of them a drink before they ordered lunch. 'What made you pick Adelaide, of all places?'

'About the same as you. This is where the job was,' Helen smiled. 'And from the look on your face I gather you're not exactly enamoured of the place.'

'It isn't Hobart,' he replied. 'But it's all right, I suppose. And with only a month more to get through, I think I'll cope okay . . . especially now.'

There'd be no prizes for guessing what he meant, Helen thought. But allowed him to continue his campaign anyway. She did enjoy his company, even if he'd have bored her sufficiently by the time he had to return to Hobart that she knew she wouldn't be sorry to see him go.

They made a date for dinner the next evening, and during the next three weeks Helen saw a good deal of the tall, blond salesman.

He was pleasant, easy, undemanding company, content in Helen's presence not only because he liked her, but because he was genuinely—surprising to Helen—lonely away from his own home city.

Looking at it, it wasn't surprising Geoff had proven so successful in Tasmania, where he'd spent his lifetime gathering contacts and learning the life-style from the ground up. But it was surprising to see that the confidence which was so evident on his home ground seemed to fade rapidly when he was in unfamiliar surroundings.

He never seemed to stop talking about Tasmania,

and by inference his presence was a continual reminder of her own visit . . . and of Dane Curtis.

Then, in the week before Geoff was due to return to Hobart, in the week Helen knew she'd be hard-put to divert him from a determined effort to convince her to go with him, there was another reminder of Dane, one she knew would be less easy to cope with.

It was Geoff that pointed out the advertisement to her, expressing his surprise that she hadn't seen it before him. 'Don't you even read your own paper?' he asked. 'I'm surprised at you missing this, anyway.'

This was an advertisement about Dane's visit the next week as part of a round-Australia tour to promote his latest published book. It wasn't the one he'd finished just before her departure, Helen knew, but the one before that, only now emerging from the year-long gestation in publishers' and printers' and proof-readers' hands.

Helen felt her heart lurch at the sight of his photograph, felt her throat constrict as her eyes took in the list of shops where he'd be available to sign copies of the book.

And of course he'd be giving press interviews as well; for one joyous instant Helen was supremely grateful that her job was at the sub-editors' desk, and not on the street as a reporter.

'I'm almost sorry I'll miss it,' Geoff mused. 'It would be a great hoot to drop into one of those bookshops and beard the lion in his den, I reckon. Dane hates the publicity part of his work so much. He never does it in Hobart, probably only does it here on the mainland because he can be sure of not running into people he knows.'

'Ah, but Marina will be in her element,' Helen muttered, as much to herself as to Geoff. And wondered at the queer look he shot her upon hearing the comment, then passed it off as surprise that she'd so blithely mentioned the name of the woman who'd won the increasingly-famous author.

They were on their way to lunch when the conversation took place, and Geoff seemed strangely pre-occupied throughout the meal. But he waited until they were dawdling over coffee to bring up the subject again.

'Why did you think Marina Cole would be involved in this publicity gimmick?' he asked without preamble, causing Helen to lean back in surprise. And he didn't wait for a reply, but continued, 'Is she something to do with why you're here . . . why you left Hobart?'

'Not really,' Helen lied. 'I got this job and I came, that's all. But surely she'd be with Dane on a trip like this . . . wouldn't she?'

'I sure as hell can't imagine why,' was the astonishing reply. And then, with a candour and perceptiveness quite unexpected from Geoff, 'And she *was* involved in your leaving, wasn't she? I don't know how, but somehow. And probably somehow not very nice, at that.'

'I've already said that she wasn't. What do you want, a sworn affidavit?'

'What I want,' he said with a grin, 'is now—I see— quite impossible.'

'And just what is that supposed to mean?' Helen asked, now genuinely puzzled. This wasn't the easy-going, comfortable Geoff Jones she thought she knew. There was a hardness to him now, a sharpness she'd never realised existed.

Then he grinned. 'Let's just say that I'd rather foolishly entertained some . . . ambitions . . . that I see now I shouldn't even have considered. Hell, I must have been blind. It's Dane, isn't it? Always has been . . . probably always will be.'

Helen said nothing. She couldn't deny it, and was damned if she'd admit it aloud, even to herself. She'd spent too many lonely nights trying to convince herself otherwise.

Geoff, unfortunately, wasn't to be put off by mere

silence. 'Helen, we've had some great times and I think we're good friends, so I'm not trying to rub your nose in this, believe me,' he said. 'But if you let that bitch Marina con you into leaving Hobart, you were dumb ... really dumb. Whatever she said to you, or did, she was lying; I can guarantee you that. That woman doesn't know what the truth is. And if she told you she had Dane all tied up and ready for shipping, forget it!'

He paused then, dramatically, deliberately, before continuing. 'I've already seen that you don't read your own paper, and you obviously haven't been following the *Mercury*, either, or you'd have seen the paragraph last week in the society pages about our Marina running off with some wealthy British yachtsman.'

Helen sat in stunned silence, unwilling to admit the rush of hope his comment had sent through her. And when she finally did speak, it was in flat tones of denial, unfeeling and totally noncommittal.

'I'm sorry, but I don't see what any of this has to do with me.' And she meant it. Apart from the sharp stab of satisfaction at hearing how Dane might himself have been betrayed ...

'Well, you just keep telling yourself that,' Geoff said, and then, finally, thankfully, dropped the subject. And as the day of Dane's arrival in Adelaide drew nearer, Helen wished desperately that she could do the same.

It served him right, she told herself, to have had Marina desert him for somebody else. If someone as unastute as Geoff could so accurately judge her character, then Dane had nobody but himself to blame if he'd let the brunette lead him down the proverbial garden path.

Helen had dinner with Geoff the evening before he flew back to Hobart, and enjoyed the evening immensely. Mostly, she decided, because he neither mentioned Dane nor Marina, and because he'd returned to being his usual, carefree, uncomplicated self. He flirted unashamedly with her, indifferent to her refusal to take him seriously, and when he kissed her good night it was the asexual kiss of an older brother.

She didn't get to see him off at the airport; at the very moment his plane departed, Helen was standing flustered and astonished in her editor's office.

'Me? No, I'm sorry but I couldn't possibly,' she managed to splutter after the initial shock of his request had worn off.

'I can't imagine why not. You do know the man; in fact he was among the references you gave. Why the hell shouldn't you interview him? Really, Helen, I'm not asking for some flamboyant exposé, just an interview in a bit more depth than anybody else is going to be able to manage.'

'I'm sorry, but no, I can't,' she repeated. 'We're old friends, and it would be just impossible. Besides, I'm sure you realise that there's nobody harder to interview than another journalist, and ... well ... because we're friends it would be even worse. I wouldn't get you a better story; I'd be lucky to get you any story at all.'

'Is there something personal between you two that I don't know about? Is that it?'

Damn the man for his perceptiveness, she thought. And replied, 'No ... or rather yes! We're ... old friends, as I said. And we used to work together, that's all.'

'And you were staying with him when this job came up?' He didn't need to ask, Helen realised. He knew!

'Yes,' she admitted, determined to admit no more than she must, and above all not to give in to this horrendous request. She just couldn't.

The editor wasn't so easily dismissed. 'You were staying with him ... five, six weeks ago. And now you don't even want to see him. That's strange, isn't it?'

'I didn't say I didn't want to see him,' Helen cried. 'I said I didn't want to be sent out to interview him, which is vastly different. And I won't interview him; I'm sorry but I just couldn't because it wouldn't work. Please don't try to make any more of it than that.'

'I see.' He took a moment to stoke up his pipe, all the time dissecting Helen with eyes that revealed far too much knowledge for her own taste. 'Do I take it then that you will be seeing him while he's in Adelaide?'

'No!' It was out before she even thought, and she had to scramble both verbally and mentally to talk herself out of the corner. 'I—that is—I don't know. I'm just not sure.'

'But of course you haven't got a specific reason *not* to see him.'

'Not really, no. Except that I know he doesn't really like the publicity aspect of things; it might embarrass him to be forced into dealing with . . . with somebody he knows.'

'Forced?' He laughed, the sound somehow grating in the quiet of the editorial office. 'My dear Helen, it will be a frosty Friday in hell before Dane Curtis is forced into anything he doesn't want to do. As I'm sure you well know. And the purpose of the exercise, may I remind you, is to promote his latest book. Nobody's forcing him, except perhaps his publishers, and even they wouldn't be sending him out on the publicity trail if he didn't want to go.'

'That isn't the point,' Helen replied, staunchly determined. She would *not* be coerced into interviewing Dane. She wouldn't go to see him, she wouldn't even buy his damned book. He was out of her life now and he could stay there.

'All right, it isn't the point. And if you want to refuse, I suppose I can't force you, because you're just as stubborn as Dane,' the editor finally conceded. Then smiled, as if that gesture alone could alleviate the suffocating feeling his proposal had surrounded Helen with.

'But even if you won't be seeing him'—and he raised one hand in a gesture to stop her interrupting—'*I* certainly will, because he and I are both old friends, too. Which leads to the obvious question—are you here? Do you exist? Or do you want to stay ... well, let's call it *in hiding*, until he's left town?'

'I ... oh, let's face it; I'd rather not meet him, if that's what you mean,' Helen finally admitted. 'But I'm not *in hiding*; I'd just rather, well, not see him. Is that so awful?'

'Nope! Not so long as I know. And you might as well know that I won't lie to him, either. All our little talk does is ensure that I won't volunteer anything. If he wants to know about you, he'll have to ask.' Then his attitude softened, becoming almost paternal. 'Tell me, my dear, does he even know you're in Adelaide?'

'I don't know,' Helen said. 'I don't think so, not that it matters. But thank you for taking this attitude; I mean that. I'm just sorry I couldn't be more co-operative, but ...'

'But, as you said, it wouldn't have made for a very good interview,' her editor said gently, smiling his acceptance. 'And don't worry; I'll try not to dump you in it when I see Dane. Good journalists are too hard to find.'

Helen left the office on shaky legs, and spent a sleepless night wondering what to do the next day. She didn't want to see Dane; she told herself that. And kept telling herself even as she strolled hesitantly towards the bookshop where she knew he'd be during her lunch break. Surely, she thought, there'd be a crowd, at least enough people for her to lose herself among them, ensure he wouldn't see her.

And what could it matter? There were no feelings for her; there obviously never had been. You didn't betray somebody you cared for, she told herself, and certainly not in the way he'd betrayed her. Something personal she might have understood, but to mess with somebody's career ... that was unfor-givable.

She actually got to within a few steps of the shop before her courage failed her, before she turned and retreated in a shambling run, half-blinded by tears of frustration as she returned to her office and hid in the masses of work that cluttered her desk.

That evening, she dined alone in a strange restaurant to avoid being home alone, then took in a movie. It was nearly midnight when the taxi deposited her at the flat, and she was groggy with nervous tension and the sleeplessness of the night before.

But the grogginess evaporated when a shadowy but familiar figure stepped forward to hand her out of the taxi, that hand remaining like a handcuff on her wrist.

'Damned well time you got home,' said Dane Curtis. 'We'll talk upstairs, eh, dear Helen.'

As he half dragged her into the entryway to the flat, Helen muttered a scathing deprecation against her new editor, only to have Dane laugh almost boyishly, although not releasing her wrist.

'You misjudge the man, Helen,' he chuckled. 'He lied, and lied and damned near ruined dinner with the bulldust he was spreading, but no, it wasn't our friendly neighbourhood editor who told me. *He* lied, but he forgot to clue in his staff; a typical mistake. Not that it mattered, really. I knew you were somewhere in Adelaide, and I'd have found you sooner or later, too.'

They entered Helen's flat, Dane reaching out in autocratic fashion for the key and Helen mutely, almost blindly, putting it into his hand. Once inside, he locked and bolted the door, turned to take Helen's coat, then directed her to the sofa with a gentle but distinct shove as his eyes prowled the room as if looking for burglars.

Helen sat silent. He looked so . . . so angry. As if he were ready to kick out at something . . . her? And so forbidding, despite his chuckle at telling her the editor hadn't betrayed her confidence after all.

'You stay there,' he said, and she did . . . sitting like a statue while he stalked through the small, tidy flat, opening closets, poking in drawers, everything but look under the bed.

And when he returned, his eyes were like ice chips as he stood like some barbaric statue himself, staring down at Helen in icy wrath.

'All right,' he said grimly. 'Where the hell's that damned Geoff Jones? Or has the rotten little bastard run out on you already?'

CHAPTER TEN

HELEN sat and stared up at him, totally unnerved by the glare of genuine anger in his frosty eyes. And when she finally did manage a reply, it emerged in a squeak of tremulous protest.

'He's in Hobart, I presume. Where would you expect him to be?'

Dane sneered, his lip curling in angry contempt. 'Here, of course. So he *has* already abandoned you, has he? Well I'm hardly surprised, except at you getting involved with him in the first place. Damn it, Helen, I thought you had better taste.'

'Better taste? What in God's green earth are you on about?' she cried. 'And why should Geoff be abandoning me? You don't make any sense at all.'

'Oh don't I? Well I suppose to you I don't, seeing you're pretty good at abandoning people yourself,' Dane snapped, eyes blazing, the muscles at his jaw fairly snapping with his anger. 'And I suppose next you'll be telling me you aren't pregnant, either.'

'Well I should certainly hope I'm not,' Helen shouted, her own grey eyes now wide with righteous indignation. 'And if I were, it certainly wouldn't be Geoff's fault.'

'The hell you say!' Dane stepped forward, one fist raised in a gesture so frighteningly dangerous that Helen flinched back against the bolster of the settee. 'Bloody hell, woman ... how many men did you manage to seduce in Tasmania? And if he isn't the father, what's the logic of running away with him? Go ahead, answer that one?'

'Answer it? How can I answer it? I don't even know what you're talking about,' Helen screamed. 'And why

178

the hell should I answer anything to you? You're a fine one to be making accusations, no matter how bloody ridiculous they are.'

'Ridiculous? I don't think there's anything bloody ridiculous about it,' Dane ranted. 'I talk to you one night, during which I might remind you there was a distinct admission that you were pregnant and that indeed I knew the father, and the very next day you run off with that tow-headed little twit, leaving me a totally incomprehensible letter, you spend damned near six weeks shacked up with him here in Adelaide and you've got the nerve to say I'm being ridiculous?'

'I have not!'

'You did so! You just said my accusations were ridiculous.'

'Well, they are! But I didn't shack up with Geoff Jones or anybody else here in Adelaide. How dare you even suggest such a thing.'

'Oh, come on ... you both left the same morning, taking care to leave Tassie on separate planes, of course. But you left together and you arrived here together and you've been together ever since. Until today, at least. What happened? Did Geoffy-baby find out I was coming to town and run for cover? He'd better have, because when I get my hands on him, he'll wish he'd never been born.'

Helen couldn't believe it. She'd seen Dane angry before, but he wasn't a violent person; never had been. And to see him now so strung-out that the slightest physical gesture might turn him into a fighter ... it was just as well Geoff Jones wasn't here. And what logic to explain that he had, in fact, only ever set foot in this flat once! And on that occasion he'd had a cup of coffee, behaved himself impeccably, and left without the slightest problem.

She breathed deeply, then slowly and deliberately spoke. 'Dane, I have not been shacked up with Geoff Jones or anybody else. I am not pregnant. I have not been pregnant. I couldn't be pregnant. I ... I just couldn't.' The final words trailed off as she shook her head in bewilderment at his anger, at the whole ludicrous situation.

'What? All that subterfuge and then you couldn't bring yourself to sleep with him after all?' The voice was scornful, but he shook his head as if in sympathy. And then the scorn was gone too, replaced by a bitterness so vivid Helen could almost taste it. 'But of course, I'd forgotten. You're a modern girl, aren't you? So it wasn't a matter of sleeping with him; just one of taking the appropriate precautions.'

Helen simply didn't know what to reply. It obviously didn't matter what she said; Dane was convinced, and nothing short of a miracle would change his mind. And, she thought, why should she bother to do that? All this was none of his business and he had no right at all to be making her the subject of such a male chauvinist inquisition. He had no right!

'I think you'd better go now,' she managed to say, holding her voice carefully under control despite the tremors that shook her slender body.

'I've only just got here. And damned if I'm going anywhere until I've got the answers I came for.'

'Until you've got the answers *you* want to hear. Whether they're the truth or not, of course, isn't relevant at all.'

'I know the truth when I hear it; you never could lie to me, Helen—and I suggest for your own good that you don't start now.'

'My own good? That's a laugh. And as for knowing the truth ... anybody with your warped sense of honesty wouldn't know the truth if it jumped up and bit them in the backside. You've got a bloody nerve standing there demanding truth after the way you've acted.'

Helen's angry retort might as well have been directed at the wall. Dane seemed not to hear, not to comprehend what she was saying. 'Are you actually going to sit there and tell me you didn't come here with Geoff Jones? That you haven't been involved with him the entire time you've been here?' he asked.

'I didn't come here with Geoff, nor have I been involved with him ... in the way you mean,' Helen replied. 'I came here to do a job. Nothing more. I didn't even know Geoff was in Adelaide until a fortnight after I arrived. Not that I expect you to believe that; in fact right now I couldn't care less what you believe. Now will you please go?'

'I've already answered that question,' he replied stolidly. 'Now it's time you provided some answers. And straight ones, for a change. You say you're not pregnant, you haven't been pregnant, and you're not involved with Geoff Jones. Now if that's the case, just what the hell is your excuse for running out, doing a total disappearing act only hours before I got back to Hobart?'

Helen didn't reply. She managed to meet his angry gaze with a sober, steady look of her own, but she didn't say a word.

'Well? You must have some excuse. And don't try to hand me a lot of garbage about the job, either, because we both know there was no reason you had to take the exact flight you did. You were deliberately avoiding me, and I want to know what it was that made you so afraid to tell me to my face.'

'I left you a letter that explained,' she replied, only to have him snort in angry disagreement.

'You left me a letter that explained nothing. Nothing! Now what was the real reason? I know you didn't make off with the silverware or anything, and you made damned sure the animals were properly cared for ... so *what*?'

'I would have thought the reason was patently obvious,' Helen replied, then snapped her mouth shut, making no attempt to be any clearer than that.

'If it was so damned obvious, I wouldn't be here asking, would I?' he replied. 'Oh, no, Helen. You were running from something. And I'll know what it was before I leave this room, I promise you that.'

Helen sat mute. You'll be here a long time, then, she thought, but mentally determined not to give him the slightest satisfaction.

Dane, after enduring her silence for what seemed like an hour, finally snorted in disgust and turned away to fling open her modest liquor cabinet, jingling bottles and glasses haphazardly as he poured each of them a drink. Helen noticed that he didn't so much as bother to ask her if she wanted a drink, much less ask what she'd prefer. She got her usual vodka-lime-and-soda.

Dane sipped at his drink, then sat down across the room from her, his eyes locked to her own as if by chains. 'Well?' he finally demanded. 'Let's have it.'

'Have what?' she replied. 'There's nothing here for you, even if I do notice that you just take whatever you want anyway.'

'Let's have the reason you scarpered without having the guts to explain to me face-to-face,' he replied, angrily but calmly enough. 'It's what you did. We both know it. Now tell me why.'

'Maybe it's none of your business,' Helen said, knowing it sounded evasive . . . knowing it *was* evasive, but unable to say much else. Obviously he wasn't going to listen when she ordered him out, and he wasn't going to listen to the truth about his own accusations.

'Of course it's my business,' he said. 'Quite obviously the whole performance is because of something I did— or something you think I did, or said or something. Although why you couldn't wait until I got back and then ask for an explanation, I can't possibly imagine.'

'Maybe I didn't need an explanation,' she cried. 'Maybe I already knew the answers. Maybe I was just totally sick of being . . . of being manipulated like some puppet.'

'The man hasn't been born yet that can manipulate you, dear Helen,' was the astonishing reply. 'And I, for one, am too smart to try.'

'Like hell!' The vehemence of her response surprised even Helen, but how could he have the audacity to say such a thing?

They sat there, glaring at each other like two pugnacious stray dogs, but it was Dane who finally broke the silence. 'You were saying?' he asked in a mild voice, speaking so softly Helen barely heard him.

'How dare you say you wouldn't try to manipulate me?' she flashed. 'You're doing it now, damn you. You've always done it. You manipulate everybody, but especially me. And how you can have the sheer gall to deny it, when I've got proof and you damned well know I have . . .'

'Proof?' His interruption was in that same low, quiet voice, but it was charged now with alertness. 'What proof?'

It was all too clear to Helen that she was being baited, being deliberately challenged in such a way that he'd get the answers he'd come for, but her flash-point anger betrayed her. She gave in to it.

'Proof? I'll give you proof,' she snarled, reaching out to yank open a drawer in the coffee table beside her. The drawer flew out, landing with a thud on the carpet, contents flying all over, but her trembling fingers quickly sorted out her proof and she flung the handful of letters across the room at him.

'There's your damned proof,' she cried. 'My job applications that you deliberately didn't mail. And don't bother to deny it, because I know better. You knew how much I needed a job, how much I was counting on those letters. And you didn't mail them, you deliberately gave me the impression I could trust you and then you did that! You lied to me. You did! You deliberately damned well toyed with my career, and don't bother to deny it because there's your proof.'

'Ah,' he said, voice so low she almost missed the sigh. 'So that's it. Well, there was a very good reason for that, although I suppose you never thought of it.'

'Oh, yes,' Helen sneered. 'An excellent reason—from your own selfish point of view. I thought of it; I even know what it was. You thought you needed me there on the farm more than I needed a job, that's what the reason was. All pure selfishness, and not one damned thing else.'

Dane, infuriatingly, only shrugged. 'I wanted to keep you with me,' he said. 'And I suppose there was an element of what might be called selfishness, but it wasn't what you seem to imagine. Not at all.'

'Not at all? It was nothing else, and I don't think that, I *know* it! You deliberately manipulated and schemed to keep me from getting a job. To keep me there on the farm to look after your animals, your home—just so you could trot off on a marathon sex orgy with your brunette friend—and you say it wasn't selfish? Well let me tell you . . .'

'What in God's name are you talking about?' Dane shouted, his voice drowning Helen's diatribe. He was on his feet, looming over her, then one hand had crushed the neckline of her dress as he lifted her to her feet, held her there, her eyes inches from his own. 'Just where the hell did you get such an insane idea?'

But before she could gasp out any sort of answer, he lowered her gently back into her seat and, with eyes shut as if in agony, whispered the answer himself. 'Marina! I should have known . . . I should have at least guessed. That bitch! That bloody scheming, interfering, rotten, lying woman.'

Dane flung his hands up to cover his eyes, and added, 'You don't even have to tell me the details; I'll bet you anything I can give them to you chapter and verse.'

And proceeded to do so without error, finally concluding, 'What I can't understand is how anybody could have the sheer bitchiness to twist it all up like she did—so deliberately and with absolutely nothing to gain.'

'Maybe she wasn't properly impressed with your performance in Melbourne, considering she didn't take long before running off with somebody else,' Helen muttered scathingly. 'Maybe you're losing your touch.'

To her surprise, Dane looked at her after that comment and suddenly burst out laughing, and even though there was a rueful tinge to the laughter, she could tell he really did think that *something* was funny.

'Losing my touch. That's the understatement of the year,' he said in a voice now strangely void of anger, even of bitterness. 'I sure as hell did lose my touch, trusting that two-faced bitch when what I should have been doing was trusting my own instincts ... and my feelings about you. All of this could have been avoided if I'd just had more faith.

'No,' he said when Helen made to interrupt. 'No, let me finish what I have to say now. It'll make everything clear, my love, never worry. Yes, I did meet Marina in Melbourne. But purely by accident—at least on my part. I'm not too sure about *her* part, with the benefit of hindsight, but it was certainly an accident as far as I was concerned. And we went for lunch, which is hardly unusual, and because I thought she was my friend, I found myself telling her things that maybe I shouldn't have. Hell, things I obviously shouldn't have, looking back.'

And he grinned at Helen, the gesture taking her back to when they'd first met, almost, to when they had definitely been—in her eyes—good friends.

'It's your fault, that,' he chuckled. 'If I hadn't been missing you so much, maybe I wouldn't have confided in Marina.'

And before Helen could begin to comprehend that statement, he held up a hand in a gesture that defied interruption, then went on, speaking quickly, positively.

'What I was doing in Melbourne, by the way, was delivering the latest book and setting up the itinerary for the current tour to promote the one just published. And what I told Marina was that I would have to find somebody competent to look after the place because I wanted you with me on the tour.

'I had hoped it would be a sort of honeymoon,' he added, and grinned even wider at Helen's gasp of understanding. 'But of course I hadn't got round to asking you, mostly because I was still, up until I got to Melbourne, just a bit unsure of whether it was fair to even ask you, considering . . . well, other things.'

'You what?' Helen couldn't believe what she'd heard. She was on the edge of her seat; then she was across the room to meet him as he rose with arms outstretched to her.

'I wasn't sure,' he said, softly, now, his lips at her ear. 'Which is ridiculous, I know, considering the whole reason I brought you to Tasmania was to give you a chance . . . to give *us* a chance. Lord, I don't know what was the matter with me, but I just couldn't—then—find the words to explain it to you. Too many ghosts, I reckon. I kept feeling that Vivian might come between us, and that our ages . . . and the brother-sister thing. Just too many ghosts.'

'Not the least of which was one with dark hair,' Helen growled into his throat. 'And that's what she'll be if I ever get my hands on her. She knew . . . she deliberately manipulated me into leaving. I can see that now. But why? How could anybody be that vindictive?'

'Hell hath no fury,' Dane muttered. 'And since you arrived, I think she finally got the message that there was no place for her in my life. I'd told her, months before you came, but I guess she saw you as the catalyst . . . oh, I don't know.'

'Well I do,' Helen whispered. 'She wanted to own you, which I see now she couldn't have done anyway, any more than I could.'

'*You* could. Very easily,' Dane replied, holding her away from him so he could look directly into her eyes. 'But only if you can accept and understand why I played such a dirty trick with your job applications. I just didn't want you to leave; it's that simple. But not because of your work ... because of you! Because I loved you, and I wanted you so desperately to find some way of loving me in return.'

'I loved you almost from the moment I arrived,' Helen told him. 'And not the puppy love I felt ... before ... when you were a happily married man and married to a woman I loved and admired and respected. The problem was, I kept seeing ghosts too, only I thought they were in *your* closet. I've never had any doubts about my own feelings, except there when I thought you were ... oh, Dane, I should have known you better. If I hadn't been so tangled up in my own feelings, I would have seen through that woman's scheming.'

'We were both misled. And by an expert,' he replied grimly. 'Because of course you can guess who tipped me off to Geoff Jones' coincidental departure for Melbourne ... after, of course, she was aware that you'd done a bunk without leaving me enough explanations. I knew you were here; it took only a 'phone call to figure out that much. But I never would have even thought of Geoff without a little help from Marina.'

'And you really thought I could run off with a, with Geoff Jones?' Helen sighed. 'Oh, really.'

'Well, he's a good-looking, likely lad,' Dane said. 'Up-and-coming, all that sort of thing.'

'He really is quite charming,' Helen said, hiding the grin by tucking her head against Dane's shoulder. 'But he's ... well he's a lightweight. And he's so young; I quite prefer mature men myself ... or at least one mature man.'

'Even a rather jealous one who's losing his touch?'

Dane asked, holding off her reply with a gentle touch of his lips, a touch that quickly became a torch to light the fires inside her.

'I hardly think I'd call that losing your touch,' she whispered when he finally relinquished her lips. 'And as for being jealous ... well I ask you—what good is a fancy sports car on a farm?'

Their shared laughter was, she thought, just the right sort for a new beginning. Dane obviously thought so too, but when it was done there were some practicalities to be considered.

'Your boss is going to have my guts for garters,' he said after yet another tantalising kiss. 'Although I suppose you could stay on here while I finish my tour. We can't be married in any event without going home to Tassie. Mrs Bowen would never forgive us, for one thing, and for another there's a mandatory one-month waiting period.'

Helen leaned against him, feeling the heat of him through her clothes, feeling the need, the love, the matching of her own passion. Her fingers laced round his neck, drawing his gaze down to meet her own.

'You might be able to wait a month,' she whispered, 'but I certainly can't. . . . I'm going with you on the rest of the tour and just you dare try to stop me. And as for my *ex*-boss, you can invite him to the wedding.'

Dane's answer was a silent, but none the less emphatic, agreement.

 **ROMANCE**

Next month's romances from Mills & Boon

Each month, you can choose from a world of variety in romance with Mills & Boon. These are the new titles to look out for next month.

MERRINGANNEE BLUFF Kerry Allyne
IMPETUOUS MARRIAGE Rosemary Carter
FANTASY Emma Darcy
THE TROUBLE WITH BRIDGES Emma Goldrick
WHO'S BEEN SLEEPING IN MY BED? C. Lamb
COME NEXT SUMMER Leigh Michaels
RETURN TO ARKADY Jeneth Murrey
AT THE END OF THE DAY Betty Neels
A PROMISE TO DISHONOUR Jessica Steele
EXECUTIVE LADY Sophie Weston

Buy them from your usual paperback stockist, or write to: Mills & Boon Reader Service, P.O. Box 236, Thornton Rd, Croydon, Surrey CR9 3RU, England. Readers in South Africa-write to: Mills & Boon Reader Service of Southern Africa, Private Bag X3010, Randburg, 2125.

Mills & Boon the rose of romance

New from Violet Winspear, one of Mills and Boon's best-selling authors, a longer romance of mystery, intrigue, suspense and love. Almost twice the length of a standard romance for just £1.95. Published on the 14th of June.

The Rose of Romance

Mills & Boon

Take 4 Exciting Books Absolutely FREE

Love, romance, intrigue... all are captured for you by Mills & Boon's top-selling authors. By becoming a regular reader of Mills & Boon's Romances you can enjoy 6 superb new titles every month plus a whole range of special benefits: your very own personal membership card, a free monthly newsletter packed with recipes, competitions, exclusive book offers and a monthly guide to the stars, plus extra bargain offers and big cash savings.

AND an Introductory FREE GIFT for YOU.
Turn over the page for details.

As a special introduction we will send you four exciting Mills & Boon Romances Free and without obligation when you complete and return this coupon.

At the same time we will reserve a subscription to Mills & Boon Reader Service for you. Every month, you will receive 6 of the very latest novels by leading Romantic Fiction authors, delivered direct to your door. You don't pay extra for delivery — postage and packing is always completely Free. There is no obligation or commitment — you can cancel your subscription at any time.

You have nothing to lose and a whole world of romance to gain.

Just fill in and post the coupon today to MILLS & BOON READER SERVICE, FREEPOST, P.O. BOX 236, CROYDON, SURREY CR9 9EL.

Please Note:- READERS IN SOUTH AFRICA write to Mills & Boon, Postbag X3010, Randburg 2125, S. Africa.

FREE BOOKS CERTIFICATE

To: Mills & Boon Reader Service, FREEPOST, P.O. Box 236, Croydon, Surrey CR9 9EL.

Please send me, free and without obligation, four Mills & Boon Romances, and reserve a Reader Service Subscription for me. If I decide to subscribe I shall, from the beginning of the month following my free parcel of books, receive six new books each month for £6 60, post and packing free. If I decide not to subscribe, I shall write to you within 10 days. The free books are mine to keep in any case. I understand that I may cancel my subscription at any time simply by writing to you. I am over 18 years of age

Please write in BLOCK CAPITALS

Signature _____

Name _____

Address _____

_____ Post code _____

SEND NO MONEY — TAKE NO RISKS.

Please don't forget to include your Postcode.

Remember, postcodes speed delivery. Offer applies in UK only and is not valid to present subscribers. Mills & Boon reserve the right to exercise discretion in granting membership. If price changes are necessary you will be notified

EP86

6R   *Offer expires 31st December 1985*